GRAVITY:
A FAIRY TALE

SARAH ALLEN

Written by Sarah Allen

Edited by Jennifer Murgia

Illustrated by Marie Delwart

Formatted by Sue Balcer

Cover Art by Miblart Designs

.

:

Also by Sarah Allen

The Fairy Tale Physics Series

Newton's Laws: A Fairy Tale
Fluid Mechanics: A Fairy Tale
Light: A Fairy Tale

Physics Story Games

The Case of the Seven Reflections:
A Fairy Detective Optics Mystery
The Sorceress of Circuits:
A Steampunk Electricity Adventure

Stick Figure Physics

Electric Circuits
Momentum
Rates of Change
Work, Energy, and Power
Basic Fluid Dynamics
The Complete Stick Figure Physics Tutorials

Math Books

Practical Percentages
Algebra 1: Exponents and Operations
Algebra 1: Foiling and Factoring

TABLE OF CONTENTS

Gravity: A Fairy Tale

Chapter One:
Too Many Kitchens

ONCE upon a time, there was a girl called Worry. On the day Worry was born, her fairy godmother appeared, pronounced her name, and then promptly disappeared. She was never heard from again.

This caused many problems for Worry.

Worry grew up in a magic castle, a school for those named by the fairies. It was run by the last remaining Scholar Knight, a formidable woman named Fortitude Knightward.

"Fort for short," she said briskly whenever she introduced herself.

However, because Worry apparently no longer had a fairy godmother, she was not allowed to use magic.

Her sister, Hope, was allowed to use magic. She had a fairy godmother, a pink sparkly, kindly one named Rose who baked her sugar cookies every time she faced a challenge.

Hope always shared the cookies.

For several years, Fort taught Hope how to use magic, and Worry wandered the castle alone.

When Worry was five years old, she ran away, determined to find her fairy godmother. She set out with a great deal of confidence and almost no supplies. The first night, she ran out of both food and water. Soaked by unexpected rain, she huddled under a tree, shivering.

Over the chattering of her teeth, she heard something approaching through the woods. She caught the flash of an eye and what looked like fangs in the moonlight.

Her heart thundering, her hands shaking, she stared at the darkness where she'd seen the eye, pressing her back against the tree.

A wildcat materialized out of the darkness. Its eyes locked on her and it lowered its head, crouching and slinking towards her. She swung her empty bag at it and ran. It snarled, its paws tangled in the straps, and then gave chase. She threw herself through the forest, stumbling over fallen logs and scrambling through clumps of ferns, the cat right on her heels, until she careened over a cliff.

For a brief moment she felt weightless. She caught a glimpse of moonlight through a gap in the clouds, then tumbled several feet onto the rocky shore below. She heard the creature's claws scrape the stones of the cliff as it leapt after her. Closing her eyes, she curled herself into a tiny ball, bracing for impact.

Fortitude Knightward appeared in a burst of glowing light, wielding a silver sword, fighting back the creature.

Worry's arm burned with pain, but she watched in awe as Fort swung her sword in a glittering arc with one hand, sending out spirals of glowing green light with the other. Fort's fairy godmother, Fern, darted this way and that, directing the energy.

At last, the creature ran. Fort turned, barely out of breath, and knelt by Worry's side.

"I'm sorry, Worry," she said, not meeting her eyes as she bent over Worry's arm, gently healing it. "I know this is hard for you."

Worry gasped and swallowed back tears. Her throat was thick. She'd made a mess. Just like usual. She hadn't found her fairy godmother; she hadn't even lasted a single night out alone.

She wanted to do what her sister could do. She knew she could do it, if they would only give her the chance.

But maybe there's something wrong with me, she thought. She wasn't like Hope. Hope was always optimistic, always helping people, lifting them up. She was always working hard. If she'd run away from home, she would have thought to bring supplies. What good was worrying to anyone, anyway?

Fort cleared her throat.

"I've been thinking. There are so many enchanted objects in the castle, and . . . I just don't have time to care for them. Would you . . . maybe . . . be willing to do that?"

4

Worry looked up suspiciously. The ache in her arm dulled, but her heart burned in her chest. *She's just trying to make me feel better.*

But Fort's expression was earnest.

It was true, there were a lot of enchanted objects in the castle, with no one to take care of them.

A lot of them were very interesting.

"Could I have my own keys?" She pointed to the iron ring hanging from Fort's belt.

Fort pursed her lips.

"Just to a few places?" Worry pressed. "Like the libraries?"

"I . . . suppose . . . as caretaker, you'd need to have your own set. To just a few places."

Worry sat up, barely noticing the pain in her arm now. There were several places in the castle she'd been curious about. More than one locked door. There was a whole room of hats, each with different magical properties. Fort had told them not to touch them, but . . . if she were caretaker . . .

Fort tilted her head, smiling at her as if reading her thoughts. She gripped Worry's shoulder, then patted it a few times.

"Very good. Well. Should we make our way back home, then?"

Worry stood, brushing some of the mud and leaves off her clothes, and nodded.

Fort gave her shoulder another firm, approving pat. She conjured a glowing ball of light and led the way along the dark beach.

Worry stared at the glowing sphere, her heart aching.

Someday, she vowed, she would go looking for her fairy godmother again. And when she did, she would be prepared.

If the only thing she could do was take care of the castle's enchanted objects, then that's what she would do.

And, for seven years, that's what Worry did.

The castle was clearly trying to be helpful. A gold-embossed sign affixed to the castle wall read "Restroom" with an arrow pointing to the left. But Worry knew better than to believe it.

She continued down the stone passage. Another sign pointing to the right read "Definitely a bathroom." It pointed to a kitchen.

A herd of silverware galloped past, pursued by a soup ladle. She turned left to avoid the Infinite Loop Corridor and cut through the Hall of Mirrors.

This was an enormous stone room with a vaulted ceiling lit by floating chandeliers. The walls were hung with ancient silver mirrors of all shapes and sizes. One showed what she'd looked like three days ago, another what she might look like in thirty years, another what she absolutely would never look like (today an iguana blinked back at her.) Honestly, it was slightly disappointing to know she'd never be an iguana.

In one corner, a tiny spoon brandished a toothpick at her from the edges of the labyrinth it had built out of corks. In the center was its prized possession, a single olive.

She paused to rummage in her pockets. Where was it? No, that was the pocket where she kept her coin collection. That was the pocket with the copies she'd made of Fortitude Knightward's keys (the ones Fort *hadn't* shared with her). That was her telescope pouch. And her leather sheath holding the maps she'd sketched of the castle, including its many secret passageways.

Ah. There it is.

The spoon danced right and left, ducking and weaving as she approached. When she bent down, it skittered away, crouching behind the tiny cork wall.

She placed the object at the entrance and moved back. The spoon darted out again but stopped when it saw her gift. Another olive. It poked the olive a few times, then did a little hopping dance, scooted it onto its head, and carted it off. Worry giggled and continued on her way.

Unfortunately, the bathroom she was most familiar with had also become a kitchen now.

She frowned, scratching the back of her head and surveying the clean new tile and copper pots hanging from the ceiling.

A crash echoed down the hallway, followed by a wail of frustration.

Worry sprinted down the hall and slid around the corner. Her sister lay collapsed on the ground.

Hope sprawled face-up, her silver hair covering her face, her pink gown pooled around her. Her fairy godmother, Rose, flitted around trailing pink sparkles.

"Marvelous, Hope, just marvelous," the fairy said, in her high, warm voice. "You're doing so well. That was amazing, darling."

Hope groaned. "It's still a kitchen."

"Oh, yes, I do see that, but it's an absolutely lovely one. Would you look at that oven! You could roast five turkeys in there!"

"I'm the worst student ever," Hope moaned.

"Well now, dear, I don't think that's quite—"

"Technically, you're the best student," Worry said.

Hope sat up, her shoulders sagging. "Oh, hey, Worry. That's kind of you, but . . . I just can't get any of this right."

"I mean, technically you're the only student, so right off the bat you're automatically the best. But even despite that, you know you're doing great. Even Fort says so."

Hope shrugged and looked down at her hands clasped in her lap. "Thanks. And I'm sorry, I shouldn't be complaining."

Worry contemplated her sister.

"How long have you been working on this?"

"Oh . . . umm . . ."

Worry turned to Rose. "How long has she been working on this?"

"Eleven hours and fourteen minutes!" Rose said brightly.

Worry took her sister's hand and hauled her to her feet. "Time for a break, then."

Her stomach twinged. She really needed to find an actual bathroom.

"You don't happen to know if there's a bathroom still left around here, do you?"

Hope slumped. "No! They keep turning into kitchens! All of them!" She glared at the gleaming copper fittings and well-stocked spice rack. "This one was so close, but it flipped at the last minute. I don't know what's wrong with this castle." She paused. "Or me."

Worry hesitated for a moment, then forged ahead. "Let me help."

Hope froze, glanced at her, then looked up and down the hall. "You can't." She said it flatly. It was the answer she always gave.

"You said you almost had it, though," Worry said, sensing an opportunity. "Rose is here. And you'd be doing most of it. I'd just help. A tiny, tiny amount."

Rose clenched her wand. "You're really not allowed. Not without a fairy godmother." She flitted anxiously back and forth. "But . . . it might be fine. Yes, I think so . . . Perhaps I should ask someone. But that could take weeks to hear back . . . No, I'm sure it's . . . fine."

Hope chewed her lips. She gave the kitchen a resentful look. "Okay, let's do it. But only help a little."

"Of course."

"And don't tell Fort."

"Never."

Hope wiped her palms on her skirts and rolled her shoulders.

"Wonderful!" Rose trilled. "Teamwork! The most noble and . . . and . . . well, that's wonderful. Assuming it doesn't go horribly awry. Which it shouldn't. I think."

Worry's heart pounded. She was going to do actual magic. She could do it; she knew she could. All this keeping her back, refusing to train her, it was silly. She mimicked Hope, rolling her shoulders and cracking her neck.

Hope whispered some quick instructions. Worry moved to stand next to her sister, and they faced the kitchen together. Rose hovered between them.

Together, they lifted their hands. Worry's fingertips tingled. Her sister's hands were full of glowing spheres of pink light. There, at the ends of her own fingertips, were tiny blue sparkles. Worry's mouth opened in wonder, which turned to a grin as she caught sight of her sister's excited smile. Hope lifted her eyebrows and together they turned back to their task. Worry's stomach felt like a hot air balloon, warm and glowing and lifting up into the stars.

"What do you think you're doing?!" The shriek pierced her concentration, and the sparkles winked out.

She whirled around to see Fortitude Knightward striding towards them, looking livid.

Her green skirts snapped around her long legs. Her black hair, a cloud of tight curls, bobbed along with her. The leather scabbard belted to her waist swung wildly, its silver pommel and bright emerald flashing.

"What are you—how many times have I warned—" Her gaze sliced through them. Fern hovered calmly above Fort's head. "I can't believe—I just can't—Do you know what tomorrow night is?"

Hope hung her head, staring at the floor. "I'm so sorry, Fort. I . . . I forgot. I've been trying to fix—"

Fort made a strangled sound and took a few deep breaths. When she spoke again, her voice was clenched. "You are . . . working . . . very hard, Hope. I know it isn't easy. It's not easy to be the last of the Scholar Knights. I . . . I know it is a great deal of pressure. Believe me."

Worry couldn't help herself. "Please let me help, Fort. I know I can do it."

Fort massaged her temple, closed her eyes briefly, and then knelt to meet Worry's gaze. "I know you want to help. That's very noble of you. But . . ."

Fort paused, tilting her head, her eyes glazing over. "Did I. . . no . . . yes, I fixed that . . ." She shook her head. "Sorry, there's a lot on my mind."

She took a deep breath. "Where was I? Right. Like I said, the syzygy starts tomorrow. The alignment of the three moons. There hasn't been one since right before my time." A haunted look passed over Fort's face. "You know that the last time, it was nearly the end of the Scholar Knights."

"What happened, Fort?" Hope whispered.

Fort shook her head. "It's better not to . . . not to say. There were only a few knights left, after." She straightened. "But that is why you must be careful. You and I are all that remains."

"Let us help, Fort," Hope said, and Worry was grateful her sister had included her.

"Thank you, but no. I have been preparing for this for years. I have many defenses ready, and I've put out a call for help. You are children. You are very talented, Hope." At this, Hope straightened, her face glowed. "But you aren't ready. And you, Worry, I'm sorry. I know you want to help, and I do wish I could teach you. But you don't have a fairy godmother. You can't be a Scholar Knight. You'll never be one."

Worry's stomach curled into a tight, cold ball.

"Please, both of you. The best you can do is to stay out of the way. Go to your rooms. Lock your doors and let no one in. The syzygy will occur every night at midnight for three nights, as the red moon joins the others. You must stay inside until it's over."

Hope nodded. "Of course, Fort. We'll do that." She elbowed Worry, who gave a reluctant nod. "It'll be okay, Fort."

"Thank you, Hope."

Fort rose in a quick, fluid motion, glancing down the hall.

"Um, Fort?" Worry asked.

"Hmm?"

Worry pointed at the kitchen.

"Right." She gave a quick nod, pointed a single arm straight at the room, and curled her fingers as if gripping an invisible ball. A tight knot of green light appeared in her fist, hovered for a moment, and then, with a rushing sound much like a toilet flushing, shot into the kitchen and exploded.

The castle shook and Worry stumbled. When she regained her footing, she looked up. Where before there had been an open archway into a kitchen, there was now a tiny, understated brown door with a brass plaque reading "Restroom."

"Thanks, Fort!" Worry shouted as she pushed the door open and dashed inside. The door was still warm from Fort's magic.

Someday, Worry thought. *Someday I'll be able to do that, too.*

Writing Prompt:

Gravity is a complex topic that took many very smart people hundreds of years to figure out. And there's still so much we don't know about it!

Over the course of this story, we'll learn what scientists currently know about how gravity works. We'll learn about orbits, tides, and the scientists who investigated them (and the many misunderstandings and misconceptions they had along the way.)

To start, think about what you know about gravity so far. Spend 5 minutes journalling about whichever of these questions interests you the most: What is gravity? Is there gravity in space? What about on the moon? Do different things fall at different speeds, and if so, why? Does the Earth experience gravity? Does gravity always point down? What does gravity feel like? What does it mean to be weightless?

Chapter Two:
The Tapestry of
Travesties

WORRY strode the short distance across her room and paused at the open window. Dark waves lapped the shore far below. Shards of light from the castle's many windows glittered off the water. The night sky was clear and star filled.

On a balcony below, Worry could just make out Fort pacing back and forth, pausing every so often to bend down and peer through her long brass telescope. It was pointed straight at the moons. The blue and the green moons were already nearly aligned. Day and night they hung in the same place in the sky, like the multicolored eyes of a giant. The red moon lifted above the horizon and slowly rose to meet them. Worry shivered.

I can't just hide in my room.

"Fort told you to stay here, huh?" Kepler asked.

The silvery, translucent ghost-cat wound around her ankles, causing goose bumps to rise on her arms. He had a sharp, pointed moustache and beard and wore a ghostly white, puffy collar.

"Yeah." Worry propped her elbows on the window ledge and rested her chin on her fists.

Kepler hopped up to join her on the sill, his tail flicking back and forth. "I'm sorry. I know you want to help."

Her shoulders slumped and she thrust her hands into her pockets. "I just want to do something."

Kepler glanced around the room. Every shelf was crammed with magical objects in various stages of repair. There were also several large piles on the floor.

"You could always organize your room."

Worry followed his gaze. "What? Why would I do that? It's perfect. Look at all this awesome stuff."

She pulled a hat out of the middle of a pile, setting off a minor avalanche. Something popped, and the smell of burned marshmallows filled the room.

She put the hat on her head, and it turned into a wide-brimmed sun hat from which tiny raindrops fell, speckling her face.

"Ah yes. Of course. Very silly of me," Kepler said.

"I just hate not knowing what's going on," Worry continued as water dripped off her chin onto her clothes. "I'm tired of being . . . just the person who's around but not doing anything. The person who doesn't know what's going on. Who can't do magic and doesn't know what's happening and isn't allowed to help."

Kepler was silent for several moments. At last, he cleared his throat. "That is very hard." He paused again and appeared to be debating whether to tell her something.

"What are you thinking?" she asked.

"Oh nothing. Only . . . You're not the only one who doesn't know everything."

"I'm sorry, Kepler. I suppose no one tells you much, either."

He cleared his throat again. "Oh, that's not what I—I know a great many things."

Worry nodded, and the rain changed to little swirls of wind, tugging at her hair.

"No," Kepler said. He sounded like he was choosing his words very carefully. "I was actually referring to Fortitude."

Worry lifted an eyebrow. "Fort's a Scholar Knight. She knew the past scholars. She knows more than anyone else. She has the keys to every room in the castle." Although, to be fair, Worry now had all the keys, too.

Kepler scrunched up his face and ran his ghostly paws over his whiskers and moustache.

"Sometimes, we think we know things, but we don't," he said, his voice strained.

Worry returned the hat to its pile. "Is there something Fort doesn't know?"

Kepler's eyes got big. He opened and closed his mouth a few times.

"Did you know that a group of jellyfish is called a smack?" he said at last.

"Huh," Worry said. She was used to Kepler's tendency to inform her of various sea facts. "Nope. I suppose Fort doesn't know that. Er . . . is there a reason she should?"

A spider scuttled across the floor, and Kepler pounced on it. The spider paused, shivered, then continued its scuttling. He batted at it with his transparent paws, then frowned.

 16

Smoothing his moustache, he glanced back at Worry, then trotted over to the door. With a single quick glance at her and a raise of his eyebrows, he darted through it.

"Kepler?" she whispered. Having never had another cat, Worry wasn't sure if this was how they usually acted. She crossed the room and placed a palm on the door, leaning her ear towards it.

Fort said to stay inside.

Worry flipped the latch, turned the knob, and slipped out into the hall.

The ghost cat had his back towards her and was staring intently up the hall. He leapt up, spun around, clapped his paws, and trotted off down the passage. He paused at the end, glancing back at her. Confused, she followed him.

They wound through the cavernous halls, past five or six new kitchens, a cluster of teapots cuddled together and snoring in an armchair, and a sign pointing down a cobwebby set of stairs that read "Definitely Not a Dungeon". Kepler continued muttering sea facts to himself. At last, he stopped right in the middle of a passage. He turned around three times, then stared up at her looking frustrated.

"Where are we going, Kepler?"

"A . . . we're going to . . . a . . . a mantis shrimp can punch so hard it breaks . . . it breaks . . . glass."

"That . . . that is pretty impressive."

Kepler's eyes were wide and pleading, though, so she knelt.

"Did you know . . . that many species of fish . . . use the . . . the ceiling to navigate?" he said.

"The ceiling? Don't you mean the sky?"

Kepler gave the tiniest of nods. He meowed. "There's a way for you to get what you want," he said again. "Everyone wants . . . to be a fish. There are so many species of fish. Clown fish are protected by anemones. But anemones would sting other . . . fish. And sometimes there are caves that go to ceilings."

Worry frowned. What was a cave that went to a ceiling? "You mean like a tower? Like . . . the old Astronomy Tower?"

Kepler immediately turned and ran in the other direction, sprinting off down the tunnel, his tail held high.

That was weird, she thought. She chewed the inside of her cheek. Why would he want her to go to the old Astronomy tower?

At least I'd be doing something besides sitting around. Fort would be angry, that was for sure. It was also the one place in the castle Worry had not been able to explore. The door to it was sealed with magic. But maybe there was a way. Or maybe Worry was going to cause something awful to happen. But maybe that thought was just a worry.

Her thoughts were getting staircase-y. And not like a grand entrance to a ballroom or a steep purposeful set of stairs up to an attic full of delightful piles of interesting objects. More like a twisting, narrow, rickety set where every third board was rotten.

She needed to know how badly this could turn out. And for that, she needed to visit the Tapestry of Travesties. Some books said it showed warnings for the future, some said it showed whatever you feared most. Some said it tried to scare you for its own amusement. When one couldn't get information, though, one could at least get harbingers of doom.

Worry felt that whatever its motives, it was better to have at least some information about what might be coming. But she tended to pay more attention to the ways things could go wrong than most people.

Her footsteps echoed in the empty halls, and she shivered. Silver symbols on the stone walls lit up as she passed, illuminating her path. Stars and planets, ancient bits of poetry.

She imagined what it would have been like, back when the halls were crowded with students and their fairy godmothers. All taking classes and learning to be knights. All with names like Courage or Elegance or Charity.

Even if I had a fairy godmother, would anyone want a knight named Worry? It was a familiar, well-worn thought. Did the world really need a champion to defend anxious thoughts? To remind people to stare out windows and imagine all the ways a possible course of action could go wrong?

She trailed her fingers across one of the thick tapestries as she passed. It depicted a dragon reading a cookbook.

The Tapestry of Travesties lurked at the end of its own dark hallway. As Worry approached, threads lifted like the heads of curious snakes, then began furiously weaving and arranging.

She clasped her hands, the keys clanking in their little sack as she brushed them. The only sound was the whisper of threads.

An image emerged. She saw herself standing alone on an unfamiliar cliff, her shoulders tense with fear, her hands balled into fists. Before her was a wide chasm, apparently bottomless (she knew this because a tiny label in cursive read 'Bottomless

Pit of Despair'). On the other side of the chasm a many-spired castle loomed, leaning to one side as if it might topple over, its windows all stained glass.

The only way to cross the chasm appeared to be a series of pendulums, giant boulders swinging towards her and away like the weights of grandfather clocks.

How strange, Worry thought.

As she watched, the threads that made up her tiny figure pulled themselves free, and Worry saw herself leap for the first pendulum. She landed on the swinging weight, but her hands slipped, and she tumbled into the chasm, her arms flailing wildly, a look of terror on her face as she fell and fell and fell.

Where was this chasm? She'd never seen anything like it. Was this what would happen if she tried to sneak into the tower? She threaded her fingers together and chewed the inside of her cheek.

Worry could easily see all the ways this could go wrong. What if a horrible monster had been imprisoned in the tower? What if she got caught? She shivered.

"I won't sneak in," she whispered to herself. "I'll talk to Fort about it again. It's better to be honest with her."

She turned around to see Hope crouching behind a statue of a gargoyle, watching her.

Chapter Three
The Forbidden Gateway

"OH. HEY..." Worry said. Hope moved out from behind the statue, glanced over her shoulder, then lifted an eyebrow at her sister. "What are you doing out here?" she whispered.

"What are *you* doing out?" Worry countered.

"Following you."

"But how did you know I was out if you weren't out already?"

Hope lifted a finger and opened her mouth, but then deflated. "Okay. I left to get some books."

"You're *still* studying? I thought you were going to take a break."

"I mean, yeah, but . . . I just needed to read a little more about what went wrong the last time I transfigured the . . . But anyway, I saw you and Kepler. So, I followed you. What are you doing? Fort said to stay in our rooms."

Worry chewed the inside of her cheek and swung her arms at her sides. She'd need magic to get in the door, anyway. Maybe she could convince Hope to help.

"I . . . I was thinking about . . . maybe . . . possibly, trying to explore the old Astronomy Tower."

Hope's eyes widened, and she rested a hand on the head of the gargoyle, but she said nothing.

Worry pressed on. "I mean, what's the difference, really, between being locked in our rooms vs. locked in the Astronomy Tower?

"Fort knowing where we are."

"Okay, yeah. But . . . I don't know. Kepler said there are things Fort doesn't know, and then hinted I should go to the tower. Or . . . I think he did."

She raised her delicate eyebrows and pursed her lips.

"I don't know," Worry went on. "It may be a terrible idea but—"

"Perfect, let's go."

Worry nearly fell over. "What?"

Hope gathered her sparkly pink skirts in one hand and turned to go. "I can't study anymore. I'm losing my mind. I can't sit around memorizing spell conjugations and waiting for some nameless horror that Fort won't explain."

"You don't think maybe we should wait for a night that's not . . . apocalyptic?"

"Probably." Hope strode down the darkened hallway, her heels clacking and the glowing silver poetry swirling and rearranging around her. "But I have a good feeling about this. Something good's going to happen, and things can't stay like this. If I see one more kitchen . . ." She raised her voice menacingly, and a doorway that had appeared up ahead hurriedly vanished.

22

Worry stumbled as she ran after her. Kepler reappeared, trotting excitedly at her side and muttering about dolphins.

The door to the Astronomy Tower was made of highly polished gray stone that looked like it was filled with smoke. Subtle colors shifted and swirled just under the surface. The only light was the faint, ghostly illumination, like moonlight, that Kepler gave off as he wove in and out of their legs.

"What's in here, Kepler?" Worry breathed.

"When threatened, sea cucumbers can eject their internal organs to entangle or distract predators," he whispered back.

"That's how I feel, too," Hope said.

Worry glanced at her sister. "Do you still want to do this?"

Her sister's face was determined as she nodded. "Yes."

Worry scanned the door, but there wasn't a knob or a latch or a knocker anywhere.

Hope reached out and placed her palm flat on the surface.

The smoke boiled and shifted under her hand, and Hope snatched it back.

Worry hunched her shoulders. She'd placed her own hands on that door many times, and nothing like that had ever happened.

Hope gasped and Worry's jealousy immediately vanished.

Words were forming on the door's surface.

> If you'd enter the tower, first stop and conspire. Like a password,
> just a pause-word, is all that's required.
>
> An anchor, an albatross, a pendulum bob.
> The pull of a planet,
> A _____ on one's mind,
> A 'hold on' homophone.

Hope frowned.

"It's a riddle," Worry said.

"What do you think?" Hope said, scratching her head.

Worry read through the riddle a few times. "Hmm . . . I think . . . I think it's a bunch of clues that all hint at the same word . . ."

She sat cross-legged, propping her elbows on her knees and resting her chin in her hands and settled down to think.

Chapter Four:
The Astronomy Tower

WORRY scratched her head. Some of the clues were words she didn't know, but she focused on what she did know.

"A _ _ _ _ _ on one's mind," she muttered. That was something she related to. A worry on one's mind?

She snapped her fingers. "I think I've got it."

Hope's face glowed. "Fantastic! What is it?"

"Weight. The word weight. A weight on one's mind. I can't remember what a homophone is, though."

"It's a word that sounds like another word. Something that sounds like 'hold on'? Oh, wait!" Hope laughed, and the bright tinkling sound echoed through the empty cavern.

They stared at the door. Hope placed her palm flat on it again. "Weight," she said firmly, and Worry felt a tingle of magic as the light around Hope dimmed and a few of her sparkles winked out.

She's so confident, Worry thought, feeling small and slightly useless. It wasn't just that Hope could do magic. She knew so many things that Worry didn't. *She deserves to do magic. She'll do good things with it.*

The grey stone dissolved, leaving the archway open.

With nervous glances at each other, they entered the tower.

They found themselves in a large, circular room dominated by a staircase that spiraled up a central column. Directly in front of them was an ornate wooden door with a heavy iron latch and—to Worry's great excitement—a keyhole.

"Hang on," she said, reaching for her bag of keys, but Hope looked longingly up the staircase.

"I'm curious how high it goes. Maybe we can see the syzygy from here."

"Just one second!" Worry said, unable to help herself. She rifled through her keys, quickly trying out a few that were of matching size and shape to the keyhole. None fit.

"Come on!" Hope urged, tugging playfully at Worry's arm.

They set off at a run up the spiraling stone staircase. The walls were hung with chalk boards, their mathematical sketches covered in thick layers of dust. Worry caught glimpses of planets, of dashed lines and hastily marked angles. Numbers were scribbled everywhere.

It wasn't long before they slowed to a jog, and then a walk, and soon they were staggering, panting and out of breath.

"How . . . high . . . can this . . . tower . . . possibly be?" Hope gasped.

"It . . . doesn't look . . . this high . . . from the outside," Worry panted.

27

They collapsed and lay gasping.

"Where'd Kepler go?" Worry asked finally.

Hope shrugged. "Probably got bored with all this climbing."

They continued staggering upwards. Worry's legs burned and sweat poured down her cheeks.

Up and up and up they went. How long, Worry wasn't sure. The continual spiraling made her dizzy, and the diagrams on the walls blurred together.

Eventually, Worry noticed something strange.

"Do you feel . . . lighter?" she asked Hope.

Hope was flushed, her silver hair damp with sweat and sticking to her head. She paused, catching her breath. "I feel shaky."

Worry attempted a bit of a jump. Her legs felt like pudding, but she could swear she was a little lighter, that she hung in the air a little longer than usual. "I really think I'm lighter."

Hope closed her eyes and rested her forehead against the wall. "It's so nice and cold." She pushed herself up. "Let's keep going. I think we're almost there."

Worry looked at the smooth stone walls, looking exactly like they had at the bottom. "What makes you say that?"

"I don't know, I just feel it."

"I think you're right," Hope said a few minutes later. She gave a slight hop. "We're definitely lighter."

"Interesting," Worry said. "I wonder why . . ."

They continued climbing. With every loop around the smooth stone, they felt lighter and lighter. As they neared the

28

top, they were taking large jumps and nearly flying up the stairs.

Why has Fort been keeping this from us?

Worry made another leap, expecting to see yet more stone around the bend, but abruptly the hall ended, and she flew out into an infinite, star-filled void. She gasped and grabbed the door frame, barely keeping herself from flying out into nothingness.

She grabbed Hope's arm as she flew past. Her sister yelped and grabbed a fistful of Worry's tunic with her free hand, pulling herself back down.

Gently, they landed on the stone surface of the tower.

They stood on an exposed platform, with only the flimsiest of guard rails around its edges. The ground was lost in thick mists far below, and above were millions of stars, like a great dome overhead. At the peak of that dome were the three moons, bathing the tower in their colorful light.

Worry tightened her grip on the door frame, glad of anything sturdy and solid to hold onto, but Hope took a tentative step towards the middle. She was nearly floating, and her step sent her gliding upwards, only just barely did she slowly drift back down. She craned her head back, staring up at the three moons as they moved into alignment, the red moon in front, blocking out the other two.

The colors shifted, and everything went red.

Worry kept her hand clamped on the door frame; her mouth open as she stared at the scene. Her sister's hair glowed red as she hopped up and floated back down, giggling.

"Worry, you have to try this!"

Worry glanced around, then pulled off her belt, tying one end to the door latch and gripping the other end firmly. She took a few steps towards Hope, bouncing upwards.

The stars glittered overhead, so much more brightly and intensely than they appeared from the ground. Worry gave an experimental jump, staring up at the moon as she did, feeling like it was drawing her towards it. What a strange feeling to be so light!

A shadow passed over the red moon. Worry's grip on her belt tightened, and she squinted.

"Worry, try this!" Hope did a little hop and a spin, somersaulting in midair.

"Hope, did you see—"

There it was again.

The shadow was getting bigger and bigger, and now Worry could see talons and great, scaly wings. Bulging amethyst eyes with red pupils. A blast of fire bloomed around the tower, filling the air with acrid smoke.

Worry lunged for her sister, grabbed her hand and yanked her back towards the door with all her strength.

Hope yelped, and the wind roared around them.

Heavy, muscular scales crashed into Worry's back and she lost her grip on the belt. She and Hope went flying towards the edge of the tower, their hands still interlocked.

A blast of flame shot over their heads, missing them by inches.

Worry made a grab for the railing, but with a horrible swooping of her stomach, she went over the edge.

30

Hope's grip on her hand tightened, and with a jolt pulled her to a stop. Worry looked up to see Hope holding onto the railing she'd missed. Hope swung Worry around, flinging her back towards the doorway.

Worry crashed into the chest of the enormous dragon perched on the tower, its mouth agape and dripping flames, its leathery wings extended, beating the air.

She drifted slowly towards its feet, then propelled herself directly between its scaly, tree-trunk-like legs. Its jaws closed in the space where she'd been only a moment ago, and she heard its teeth clang against the stone.

Pushing off the ground, she flew towards the doorway, shooting straight through it, passing a glowing comet of pink light trailing fairy dust heading the other way.

Worry spun around, grabbing the end of her belt again, wishing it were longer, and prepared to leap out to get Hope.

Hope's fairy godmother, the tiny Rose, shot past the dragon, who roared. The sound crushed in on Worry's ears. She flinched, but there on the edge of the tower, she could just see her sister's small, pale hands gripping the railing as she hung off the end of the tower. It was lucky the gravity was so low, otherwise she might already have fallen.

Rose flitted this way and that, tapping the beast with her wand and darting out of the reach of its claws. "Oh my, oh no. Stop it," she said, punctuating each exclamation with a rap of her wand. It swiped at her as if she were a mosquito, batting her away.

The dragon shot another jet of flame at Hope, and one of her hands lost its grip.

It reared its head for another blast, but Worry leapt out, still clutching the end of her belt. She grabbed one of the bags of coins and hurled it at the dragon's shoulders. It pinged off its back, and the dragon spun, its purple irises widening, the pupil contracting to a tiny, enraged pinpoint as it glared at Worry.

It opened its jaws, and Worry leapt upwards with all her strength. A blast of flame went just beneath her.

She heaved as hard as she could on the belt and went shooting back down and to the side, another blast of flame just missing her.

Around the side of the creature, Worry could just make out Hope's tiny hands, both back on the railing, as she edged her way around towards the door. *Faster, Hope.*

The sparkling pink fairy was back, heading straight for the dragon's eyes. She gave a tiny, high-pitched war shriek, but it batted her away again.

Hope was halfway around the tower now.

"Jump!" Worry yelled. "Hope, jump!"

Worry crouched; her muscles taut as she prepared to leap towards wherever Hope ended up. She'd catch her and pull them both back to safety.

She pulled another bag of coins off her belt and hurled it towards the dragon. It sailed straight into its mouth.

The dragon's eyes widened; its talons scraped at its neck. It coughed a few times, then in a great, fiery belch, the bag of coins sailed back up, the fiery remnants of the bag disintegrating and the hot coins spewing everywhere. It hacked again, pounding its chest with its talons, and belched up more flames.

Hope came flying up over the railing, overshooting a little and heading for just above the doorway. Worry leapt upwards to meet her.

They timed it perfectly. Hope wrapped her arms around Worry's stomach, and Worry yanked as hard as she could on her belt-anchor, pulling them back towards the doorway.

It was so close. Three feet, then one foot. Worry pulled them towards it as hard as she could. They were going to make it, she knew it.

Something jerked them backwards.

Worry pulled harder and harder, but she couldn't help herself. She risked a glance behind her. The dragon had a talon wrapped around Hope's ankle. She felt her sister's grip slip a few inches.

"Hold on!" Worry yelled, but even as she did, Hope slipped again. Worry let go of the belt with one hand, grabbing the shoulder of Hope's gown with the other.

Rose flitted this way and that, tapping ineffectually on the dragon and shouting at it.

But it was no use. The dragon yanked Hope out of Worry's grasp, and in a great rush of leathery wings lifted off the tower with her dangling from its claws.

Worry leapt after her sister, but just missed her tiny pink satin slippers as she was lifted away into the night.

Worry flailed her arms, just managing to avoid shooting over the edge of the tower. She stood, breathing heavily, heart pounding, as she watched the dragon stealing her sister away. They were heading straight for the red moon.

"Hope!" she yelled. But her voice was lost in the rush of wind. Worry pulled at her hair, grabbing everything out of her belt and dumping it out and letting it drift to the ground. There had to be something. Something. She had to do something.

Next to her, a tiny distraught figure flitted this way and that, trailing bursts of sparkling fairy dust.

"Oh no. Oh no no no," Rose muttered, gripping her wand in both hands and fiddling with it. "No. No this wasn't supposed to happen."

Worry looked at her sharply. "What—what do you mean? What *was* supposed to happen?" Had the fairy somehow planned this?

Rose's eyes widened, her tiny, pointed face flushed. Her wings fluttered, and she disappeared with a small pop.

Discussion Question:

Do you have any guesses about why Hope and Worry felt so much lighter at the top of the tower? Are there times that you've felt light like that? What were you doing? Next time you're on a swing set or riding in a car as it goes over a hill, or in an elevator just as it starts to go down, pay attention to what that feels like. Those are all moments where you feel a little bit weightless.

Chapter Five:
Sea Riddles and
Syllogisms

WORRY stared up at the moon, hoping to catch one last glimpse of her sister, trying to see where she went. *I'm coming, Hope. I'll fix this.*

She glared around the empty tower, still breathing heavily. "Rose!"

But no fairy appeared. An empty stillness descended, leaving the night feeling eerily calm. Only the faint smell of dragon smoke hung in the air.

Shaking, Worry swept up her belt and the few coins that were within easy reach, stuffed them into her pockets, and flew down the stairs.

Her mind was whirling. Where was the dragon taking Hope? What did Rose know? What had she meant, this wasn't supposed to happen? Fort was going to be furious, but she would fix this. She would know what to do, Worry was sure of it.

Worry collided with Fort halfway down the stairs, but the woman was a stable as a tree and Worry only bounced off her legs.

Fort knelt, picking Worry up and gripping her by the shoulders. "What are you doing here? I told you to— Where's Hope?"

Fort's green eyes bored into Worry's, and she felt herself shaking.

"A . . . a dragon," she gasped out.

Fort's grip tightened and her eyes went wide.

"Are you sure?"

"We have to do something! It took—it took . . ." She couldn't finish the sentence.

"No. No this can't be," Fort said.

"We have to get her back!"

Fort released Worry and stood, shaking her head, her hand going to her sword hilt.

"This is bad. This is very bad." She paused.

Worry had never seen Fort speechless before, but it looked like she really needed a moment to think. Worry's chest felt like an empty void. If Fort didn't know what to do . . .

Her ankles tingled and she looked down to see Kepler sitting on one of her feet.

Fort noticed him, too.

"This was your doing, wasn't it?"

Kepler gave an innocent meow and flicked his tail.

"I know you can talk," Fort said.

Kepler hissed, his hackles rising.

36

What was going on here? Worry didn't have time to try to figure it out. With every second that passed, Hope was farther away.

"Fort?" she said. "I'm so sorry. We broke into the tower. But . . . the top of the tower was so strange, and then a dragon came, and it took Hope. It was heading for the red moon. What do we do? How can we get her back?"

Fort ran a hand across her brow, looking deeply exhausted. She knelt again, and Worry noticed her hands were shaking.

"Worry, I am so sorry. But there's no getting her back. She's gone."

Worry shook her head. No. No that couldn't be.

"She's not gone! I saw where she went! She went to the red moon!"

Fort stood in one swift movement. "Worry, I'm sorry, but . . . the fact that you saw a . . . a dragon . . . well this is very, very bad." One hand went to her throat, and the other rubbed her sternum, her eyes glazing over. Worry had never seen Fort so undecided. She looked . . . afraid.

Her expression was grim. "More are coming. This is only the beginning."

"What do you mean?"

"This is what happened before. It's what nearly ended the Scholar Knights. It's why I'm the only one left."

"What can I do?"

Fort's gaze was far away. "There's nothing you can do. I wish you had hidden like I asked." Worry wished she could shrink to the floor. At last, Fort looked straight at her. "Please,

Worry. Your sister is lost, but if I don't act quickly, the rest of the world might be lost, too."

Fort's words twisted like sharp splinters in her heart. There was nothing Worry could do. She couldn't do magic; she couldn't help her sister. She'd already made things worse. She looked down at her feet and nodded.

Fort clapped her on the shoulder. Her gloved hand was heavy.

"I'm sorry," Worry said.

Without another word, Fort sprinted up the tower, drawing her sword.

Worry sank down, sitting on the steps, wrapping her arms around her knees, and bowing her head. Kepler nuzzled her hand. All Worry could think about was Hope disappearing into the night sky.

She couldn't do nothing. She couldn't hide while her sister was in danger. "I'm coming for you, Hope," she whispered, looking upwards. She said it more for herself than for her sister.

But what was she supposed to do now?

"Rose?" she whispered to the empty air. "Please talk to me."

No one answered. Only Kepler stared back up at her.

Worry heard a crash from high above and leapt to her feet. She started up the stairs again, then paused. Fort didn't want her help. She'd only tell her to go back to her room.

There was no way Worry was just going to go back to her room now, even though she'd already made things worse. She turned and sprinted down the rest of the stairs, Kepler close on her heels.

When they were out of the tower, Worry darted down a narrow passage into an unused classroom, slamming the door behind her. Kepler hopped through the closed door and stared up at her, licking a ghostly paw.

"Kepler, what is going on?" she demanded. "Did you know that would happen?"

Kepler rubbed his paws over his nose, flattening his pointed moustache. "No, of course not. I didn't know that would happen."

"What else do you know? Tell me everything."

"Sea turtles travel thousands of miles and lay their eggs on the same beach they were born."

She groaned, but really, she walked right into that one. "Why do you do that?" she demanded.

"Pufferfish expand into a ball to evade predators."

Worry grimaced. "Is there anything you can tell me that isn't sea facts?"

"Yes, of course. I don't really care for sea facts much myself."

"Then why— No, never mind, don't answer that." She pursed her lips, pacing back and forth. She had to get Hope back. To do that, she had to figure out what was going on. Because there was clearly a lot more happening here than people were telling her. Rose wouldn't talk to her, but that wasn't surprising. Fairies were very shy and often only spoke with their chosen knight.

Fort wouldn't talk to her either and that stung her more. She clearly only saw Worry as a burden.

"What is going on?" she muttered to herself, trying to hold back the panic that kept threatening to overwhelm her when she thought about Hope imprisoned by a dragon on that far-away moon.

And Kepler wasn't telling her anything useful. Although. She tapped her chin. Maybe she could figure out something from when he told her sea facts and when he didn't.

She sat cross-legged on the floor and took a deep breath. It was hard to think when everything felt so urgent. But running around panicking—which was what she'd really like to do most—wasn't going to get Hope back. Maybe she'd allow herself some running around panicking time later.

"Okay, Kepler. What are some things you can tell me that don't have to do with the sea?"

Kepler sat up straight, his eyes wide and excited, his moustache perked. "Oh, thank you, what a fantastic question." His tiny tongue licked out and back in. "Well. I could speak about the castle. About the Scholar Knights. About the sea, and the earth and the sky, but no higher. I can speak about people who look at the sea, or the earth, or the sky, but no higher."

Worry's eyebrows lifted. "Hmm . . . so, you can't talk about . . . the stars. Or the people who look at stars?"

"A giant squid eye can be up to ten inches in diameter," Kepler said, looking deeply pained.

"Wow, that's big," Worry said. She briefly wondered what it would feel like to hold one. "We have to focus," she said.

"I will focus like a giant squid eyeball focuses on a fish!" Kepler assured her.

She nodded absently. "Okay, is there anything else useful you can tell me?" It occurred to her that Kepler was the one who'd led them to the tower in the first place, so following his advice might not be a very good plan. But she'd known Kepler her whole life, and of everyone in this castle he was the only one at least trying to give her information.

"There are some books missing from the library," he commented.

This was intriguing, although she wasn't sure how she was supposed to go looking for books that weren't there.

"Can you show me?" she asked.

Kepler opened his mouth, raising a paw, but with what was clearly a lot of effort, shut his mouth again. She was slightly curious to hear what sea fact he'd managed to avoid saying.

"All right, I'll take that as a no," she said.

"Thank you. I greatly appreciate your line of questioning."

She wished she'd thought to ask him about his strange interest in the sea long before. "Have you known many Scholar Knights?" she asked.

"Oh yes, a great many," said Kepler, suddenly serious. "I was very good friends with several of them, in my youth."

She wondered what had happened but knew better than to ask by now.

A strange question occurred to her. "Were you always a cat?"

"Dolphins have unique whistle-names for each other."

Whoa. If Kepler hadn't always been a cat, what had he been?

Luckily, Worry already had an idea of where those missing books might be. The benefits of years of exploring. She wove her way through a maze of staircases, down into the enormous library. One whole wall of the library was floor-to-ceiling windows that looked out over the ocean. Right now, the ocean was dark, illuminated only by moonlight. The syzygy had passed for that night, and flecks of red, blue, and green glinted off the ocean, bathing the library with a dim, watery glow of shifting colors.

She hurried through the long rows of empty reading tables, her feet silent on the thick, dusty carpet, then wove a familiar path through the endless shelves. Back and back and back she went, arriving at last at a small, locked door.

The iron key she'd found last year fitted perfectly, and she ducked inside, coughing as she inhaled dust, and batting away the spider webs.

Inside, the room was lit by glowing magic orbs. One large, white orb hovered in the center, with three smaller orbs rotating around it. One red, one blue, one green.

"Kepler is that—" but she cut herself off, seeing that Kepler was looking determinedly away from the object. The last time she'd been here she hadn't paid much attention, had assumed it was simply a fancy magic lamp. But now it was obvious what it represented.

She approached, seeing that the red moon had moved past the blue and green orbs, which rotated together as the great pearly planet moved beneath them.

It was a model of their planet and the three moons.

The last time she'd been there, she'd opened a few of the books, but they were mostly indecipherable symbols and diagrams, and she'd given up.

She reached out and plucked the little green moon from where it hung. It was surprisingly cool. Holding it up, she moved farther into the room, sending long shadows arcing away from the green glow of the orb.

At the very back of the room was an ornate shelf set into the far wall. On it were five gold pedestals. On the first rested an ancient, leather-bound book. The other four were empty.

Engraved on the front of each pedestal was a name. She read them off one-by-one, trailing her finger over the letters.

"Aristotle. Galileo. Newton. Einstein." She paused, her finger hovering over the final name. She looked at the ghost cat, who was staring out into the ocean, but watching her out of the corner of his eye. "Kepler."

Why was there a book with the name of her cat here? Or rather, a missing book. She ran her hands over the pedestal, looking for any other engravings or maybe a secret button, but there was nothing.

Leaving that for later, she approached the first book.

The front cover was embossed with a crown of laurel leaves and the spine read 'Aristotle' in gold letters. Gently, Worry opened it.

Einstein

Galileo

Aristotle

The inside was blank: crinkly, ancient parchment, weathered and water stained, but no writing.

She flipped through a few more pages. All empty.

She paused, staring at a blank page. A tiny scrawl of ink appeared.

To speak with the Father of Logic, you must master the tools of logic.

Worry already considered herself fairly logical, except when it came to her unrealistic anxieties. She waited, and more words appeared.

Complete the Syllogisms

"Kepler, do you know what a syllogism is?" she asked, bracing for information about clams or something.

"They're logical statements. Formal logic. Usually, you're given two pieces of information, and you have to put them together. See what logically follows."

"Hmm, okay. Thanks."

That didn't seem too hard.

The words disappeared, and more took their place.

All fairies have wings.
Bluebell is a fairy.

Worry considered this. Was there anything she could conclude? If Bluebell was a fairy, and all fairies had wings, then Bluebell must have wings.

She pulled her quill and ink from her bag and, feeling slightly terrible for writing in what was probably a priceless ancient artifact, carefully wrote out *Bluebell has wings.*

A sparkling sensation went through her fingers, almost like she'd dipped them in fairy dust, and the words disappeared. She let out a sigh, grateful that her writing wasn't going to forever mar the book.

Correct.
If the tide is high, the mermaids will come close to shore.
The tide is high.

Worry chewed the end of the quill, then stopped herself. Well, it seemed there was one thing that logically followed.

The mermaids will come close to shore.

Again, her words disappeared, replaced by a new riddle:

If you tickle a giant, he will laugh.
The giant is laughing.

"Hmmm . . ." Worry wondered aloud. Her first instinct was to say that someone had tickled the giant, but . . . what if someone had told the giant a particularly good joke? He could be laughing for many reasons. She frowned and wrote out her answer.

I don't think we can conclude anything.

Words replaced it almost immediately.

Well done.

A strong smell of ink filled the room, and the pages rustled, flipping back and forth as if in a gust of wind. They filled with writing.

Some Syllogisms to Solve:

1. If you give Fort a cupcake, she will be happy. You gave Fort a cupcake.

2. All dragons have scales. Hortense is a dragon.

3. If a dragon is angry, it will breathe fire. A dragon is breathing fire.

Answers: 1. Fort is happy. 2. Hortense has scales. 3. We can't conclude the dragon is angry. Something else might be making it breathe fire. Maybe it has indigestion or is trying to re-heat leftovers.

Chapter Six:
The First Teacher

WORRY flipped through the ancient book. "Is there something in particular I'm supposed to be looking for?" she asked Kepler, but the cat only gave her a pained look and went to stare out the window into the darkness.

The pages filled with complex notes and diagrams. Arrows pointed everywhere. She paused at a detailed sketch of an octopus. There was a whole page of notes on fish skeletons, and then a long essay on virtue and how balance made one a good person. Then intricate sketches of ferns and the structures inside flowers.

Worry scratched her head. *Did one person write all of this?* The handwriting all looked the same.

One page went into detail about how to persuade others, which Worry thought she might come back to next time she tried to convince Fort to teach her to be a knight.

Fort. Her stomach flipped over as she remembered why she was here. She'd been so caught up in the logic puzzles that she'd almost forgotten Fort was off trying to prevent some secret impending disaster. And Hope had been carried away by a dragon.

She flipped faster through the pages, looking for anything that might give her a clue as to what was happening and what she should do.

At the very end, there was a nearly blank page that had only one word on it.

Hello?

Worry frowned, then she picked up her quill and scratched out a response.

Hi?

Ah, hello, the parchment answered. Worry read the words aloud, so Kepler could follow along, even though he didn't seem to be paying attention.

Who are you? she asked. The words disappeared, and more began to take their place.

My name is Aristotle. In my world I am often called The First Teacher. Some call me The Founder of Logic or The Father of Biology. I am also famous for my philosophy, my ethics, and my principles of drama.

One person could do all that?

Wow, that's a lot, Worry wrote. *How did you learn all that?*

My father was a physician. He sparked my interest in biology. From there, I became interested in a great many subjects.

Nice to meet you, she replied. *Um, how am I speaking with you?*

Many years ago, the fairies created this book and others like it to allow scholars from your world to ask me questions.

Is it uncomfortable, being a book?

Only when people ask me illogical questions. There was a pause. *But it is kind of you to ask. What are you hoping to understand?*

Worry considered whether it was safe to be writing to a talking book. But she didn't see how else she was going to rescue her sister, so she continued.

My sister was kidnapped by a dragon from the top of a tower here. The dragon took her to one of the moons. I need to figure out a way to rescue her.

I see. That sounds difficult. Tell me, what did you observe?

Observe?

Yes, what did you see? The first step in understanding anything is to carefully observe.

Worry described everything she could remember, from the lightness at the top of the tower to the fairy's exclamation at the end.

Hmmm . . . I see. Most fascinating. In my world, we have only one moon. And no dragons.

Worry chewed the end of her quill again.

What do you know about my world? she asked.

Very little, I confess. I mostly answered the astronomers' questions.

Worry frowned. *What do you mean, the astronomers? Don't you mean the Scholar Knights?*

No; the Scholar Knights weren't interested in speaking with me.

There were astronomers here?

Assuming you are in the Castle of the Scholar Knights, then yes. There was a small group of astronomers doing research there as well.

Worry's heartbeat quickened. Fort had never mentioned this group. *What did they ask you?*

They asked me about the celestial spheres and how to reach them.

Worry gripped her quill hard. The astronomers had wanted to reach the moons? Had they achieved it? If so, maybe she could do the same!

Aristotle continued, *I told them that it was impossible. Everything in nature has its place.*

Worry's heart sank. *What do you mean?*

I mean everything is composed of five elements. At first people thought there was just earth, water, air, and fire, but I added a fifth: aether, which is what the heavens are made of. Earth and water naturally move downwards. Air and fire naturally move upwards. Aether belongs in the heavens.

When Aristotle said this, Kepler growled and flattened his ears.

Aristotle went on. *Everything has its natural state. Things prefer to be stationary and will naturally come to rest without some force to keep them moving. I am quite curious about these dragons. If they truly can reach the celestial sphere, perhaps they are made of aether. It would be quite wonderous to see a creature made of aether. Perhaps your sister's natural place is also in the outer, heavenly sphere . . .*

Something about this struck an uncomfortable chord for Worry. She'd often felt like she and Hope were just fundamentally different from one another. Hope belonged someplace better than Worry. It was a horrible thought. That maybe Worry was simply like earth and water. Heavy.

She paused, her quill hovering over the page. Her throat suddenly felt thick.

Kepler batted her gently on the side of the head. She hadn't even noticed him climbing onto her shoulder. She glanced at him, and he rolled his eyes, leaping away for one of the bookshelves.

She shook her head. That was silly. Obviously, Hope hadn't wanted to be carried away by a dragon. She took a deep breath and continued.

What else did they ask about?

They asked about the tendency of objects to fall. I told them that objects that are heavier fall faster, and that they fall more slowly through thicker substances.

Kepler hissed and lashed his tail.

They also asked me about the possibility of a vacuum, of a completely empty space. I told them that was impossible, because objects would move infinitely quickly in such a space. And that would be impossible.

Worry could sort of see how Aristotle might have concluded this. It was like reasoning with the syllogisms. Objects move slower through mud than through water. The thinner the substance, the faster the object. If a substance is infinitely thin, the object will move infinitely fast. It seemed logical, on its surface. She wondered if there might be more going on, though.

Did they ask you anything else?

There was a longer delay than usual before Aristotle replied. The handwriting became messier, with little flicks and scratches and dots of splattered ink.

They did ask me quite a lot about tides. Such a complex topic. Such a regular, repeating phenomenon, but so different in different places. I . . . I think it must be the wind. Winds move waves, and . . . and they must also cause the tides.

But winds are so chaotic, Worry wrote. *Why would they blow in such a uniform way?*

Perhaps . . . perhaps from heat from the sun.

Worry considered this. It didn't seem very likely. Why had the astronomers been interested in them?

Did they ever say why they wanted to reach the moons?

Not to me. But I know they had other books. They spoke with me quite a lot early on, and then, when they had their other books, they stopped. It's been nice talking with you. I haven't had a student in a long time.

I'm sorry. There haven't been astronomers here in a long time, either. Otherwise, I'm sure they would want to speak with you.

That is very kind of you to say.

I have to go now but thank you for the information.

Of course. Best of luck to you in your quest. I sincerely hope that you are able to rescue your sister. Should she not be made of aether and destined for the stars.

Worry snapped the book shut and stared at the other golden pedestals. Aristotle had a lot of interesting ideas, but many of them seemed not quite right. Maybe the astronomers had felt the same way. Her pulse quickened, and she twirled her quill through her fingers, thinking. The silence of the room closed in on her, all sound muffled by the books and the layers of dust. Kepler crouched, darting a paw under one of the shelves, his tail flicking back and forth.

So there had been another group of people here, besides the Scholar Knights. Astronomers. Maybe these astronomers had found a way to reach the red moon. Maybe the information in the other books was more useful. Maybe someone had stolen or hidden them because of this.

The idea of travelling to the red moon, knowing there was at least one dragon waiting for her was more than a little worrying, but if there was a way to do it, Worry was going to try.

Test Aristotle's Ideas:

Aristotle was a brilliant person who contributed so much to our understanding of the world, but there was a lot he got wrong. Still, those ideas were a valuable first step in our understanding of the world, and it's easy to see why he would have concluded some of the things he did, based on what he saw in the world. The world is complicated, and we can't always perceive the factors that cause things.

In this activity, let's try to see if we can disprove Aristotle's ideas, and maybe understand what he got wrong. Firstly, let's look at the idea that heavier objects fall faster. 1. Take a piece of paper and a rock. 2. Drop them both from the same height. Which one hits the ground first? 3. Now, do the same experiment again, but this time crumple the paper up so that it is the same size and shape as the rock. 4. Drop them both from the same height. What do you notice? Do they land at the same time? Closer? You see, what Aristotle didn't consider was that objects are falling through air, which slows them down. Flatter, lighter objects are more affected by air than are the more compact, aerodynamic objects.

Aristotle believed that it was impossible to have empty space, but nowadays we are able to pump all the air out of a container using a vacuum pump. What would it really look like to drop objects in a container without air? Watch this YouTube video to see. It's pretty mind-blowing. "Brian Cox visits the world's biggest vacuum | Human Universe – BBC"

Chapter Seven:
Circles and Secrets

WORRY knew better than to ask Kepler where she might find the book with his name on it.

The cat leapt onto her shoulder again, cooling and weightless, and together they climbed the steps out of the library, bursting out into a stone hall. A gargoyle snorted awake, peering at her through bleary eyes.

"Sorry to wake you," Worry whispered, and the gargoyle hmphed, tucked its head under a wing, and went back to sleep.

Worry put one hand on her hip and rubbed her chin with the other.

Where could the book possibly be?

Another library? In a secret passageway?

Moving down the hall away from the gargoyle, Worry pulled out her maps and spread them over the stone floor. She had several of the various sprawling wings of the castle and a few more of the surrounding countryside.

The castle of the Scholar Knights was a day's ride from the nearest villages. She hadn't left the castle since she'd been brought there as a baby. Not for the first time, she wondered where she'd come from. A nearby village? Farther?

Was there some secret underground bunker filled with treasures nearby? The parchment crinkled as she ran her hands over it, peering closely at names and labels.

If there was a repository of secret knowledge, the safest place for it would probably be the castle.

She'd explored every inch of it, though. A hundred times at least. She'd found a few secret closets, yes, mostly by looking at blank spaces on the map, but she'd thought she'd found the last of them years ago.

She waved Kepler a little closer so she could use his light to read by.

Time passed, and Worry's eyes began to get heavy. She yawned widely. Her mind felt foggy, but somewhere in this castle was a book, and she was determined to find it.

"I need a break," she said finally, her vision blurry. Kepler hopped onto her shoulder and together they wandered the halls of the castle, past snoring enchanted statues.

What am I even looking for? Worry wondered as she passed under an arch of glowing purple flowers from which soft jazz music emanated.

She tapped a stone frog, then twisted it, and a passageway opened. Passing into the darkness, she was glad of Kepler's light. He'd been mostly silent, occasionally starting to mutter something, but cutting himself off.

Maybe it was time to ask Fort again. Maybe now that the first night of the syzygy was past, and the moons would be out of alignment for a few hours, she'd be more open.

The passage sloped down, and Worry walked slowly, running her hands along the walls and looking for anything out of the ordinary. Anything that might hint at another secret door. Although, she knew that on the other side of the left wall was the library and on the other side of the right wall were a series of cobwebby classrooms full of empty glass jars. But this was the tunnel she had explored the least. Mostly because it was so long and boring.

She squinted, struggling to see, and realized Kepler's light was growing dimmer.

"Kepler, wake up," she whispered.

"I am awake."

The light didn't change.

She lifted an eyebrow. "Does your light usually get dimmer?"

"I haven't noticed, to be honest."

She turned around and walked back up the hall. Gradually, Kepler's light increased. She tried it a few more times to confirm. Yes, he was definitely brighter at one end of the tunnel than the other.

Intrigued, she retraced her steps, this time watching as Kepler's light dimmed and flared. It was hard to pinpoint, though, with the twisty passages, some higher and some lower. She'd think she was onto something, with the light getting brighter and brighter, only to find herself stuck at a dead end.

She needed to be more systematic.

She retrieved the little green ball representing the moon from the library, and wandered the castle until Kepler was exactly as bright as the moon, then she marked the spot on the map.

Then she set off for a different part of the castle, wandering around there until again she found a spot where Kepler was again exactly the same brightness as the moon. Again, she marked the spot on the map.

"What are you doing?" Kepler asked.

"I have an idea," she said, heading off for a new part of the castle.

"What?"

"Let me see if it works first, then I'll explain."

Technically, she only needed three dots, but the castle was so complicated and consisted of floors and half floors and balconies and angled ramps—and who knew how accurate this map was anyway—so she added more and more, until she was certain.

Flushed and grinning, she spread the map on an oak desk below a window. The sky outside was dark, the red moon neared the horizon, about to set.

"Look!" she whispered to Kepler. "Look at the shape!"

"A circle?"

"Exactly!"

"Well done. Geometry is a worthwhile pursuit, to be sure. And, um . . . How is that helpful?"

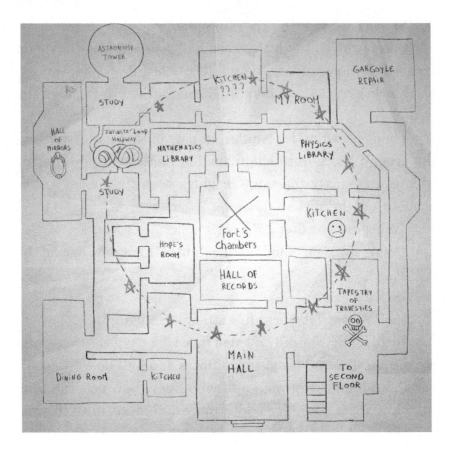

"I think you get brighter when you're closer to your book. Each of these dots is a place where you were exactly as bright as the little moon, which means you were exactly the same distance from your book."

Kepler went very still. Not even his tail moved.

"Every point on a circle is the same distance from exactly one place," she said, pausing for dramatic effect. "The center."

With a flourish, she connected the dots into a smooth circle. She peered closer, her quill hovering over the map. She poked her quill right in the middle, making a single dot on the center, and her chest tightened, her stomach turning over.

It was Fort's chambers.

The Geometry of Gravity:

There are two shapes that are particularly important to our understanding of gravity. One is the circle, and the other is the ellipse. They're both super useful for a lot of things, actually, and understanding what they are fundamentally is not only interesting but helpful later on. So let's learn to draw them!

For this activity, grab a piece of string, two thumbtacks, a piece of cardboard, and a pen. First, let's draw a circle. Place the cardboard flat on the ground. Tie the string to the pen, then thumbtack the other end to the middle of the piece of cardboard. Hold the pen upright, like you're going to draw on the cardboard, and move it to where the string is taut (not sagging). Now, keeping the string taut, use the pen to draw on the cardboard. If you go all the way around the thumbtack, you'll have a circle! By using the string, we're keeping the distance from the center to the pen constant. This way, every point on the circle is exactly the same distance from the thumbtack.

Now, let's draw an ellipse! This time, cut a length of string and thumbtack each end of it to the cardboard, making sure the string is loose in between. (The string should probably be about half again as long as the distance between the two thumbtacks.) Now, pull the middle of the string away from the thumbtacks until the string is taut. Place your pen there, holding the string in a kind of triangle shape. Now you can start to draw. Try to move your pen in such a way that the string is always taut. You should end up with an elongated circle- an ellipse! This also works well with nails. For a video of this, search on YouTube for "draw a PERFECT ellipse with a string and two nails".

So, what's the difference between a circle and an ellipse? Well, a circle is a shape where every part of it is exactly the same distance from the center. An ellipse is like a circle, but it kind of has two centers. We call each of these points a "focus." In our activity, each of the thumbtacks is a focus of the ellipse. Because we tied a string between the two of them, we kept the total distance from the pen to each of the two foci (foci is the plural of focus—like octopi and octopus,) the same. So, wherever you are on the edge of an ellipse, if you measure the distance from that point to each of the foci and then add those distances together, you'll always get the same amount. Kind of complicated, but interesting!

Chapter Eight:
Books both Judgmental
and Hidden

THE door to Fort's chambers was shiny red madrona. Its frame was a single, curved branch lifting up and back down. "Fortitude Knightward" had been artfully burned into the door's surface, surrounded by sprays of maidenhair ferns.

Worry gulped. Fort could be back any moment. What would she do if she found Worry breaking into her rooms?

She pulled a key from her bag.

"You have a key to Fort's chambers, too?" Kepler hissed.

Worry blushed and hunched her shoulders. "I know I shouldn't. I just . . . She lost it one time and we all searched for hours and hours and finally I found it and . . . I just . . . made a teeny tiny copy before returning it."

"How did you copy the key? Are you learning smelting in your spare time?"

She giggled. "No. I found this cabinet that duplicates things you put in it. Or sometimes it turns them into cupcakes."

"Seems like a risky thing to do with Fort's keys."

"True. It worked, though!" She inserted the key and, with a quick glance over her shoulder, turned it. The door clicked open. "And it's helpful to Fort, too, really. Like when she loses them again. Which she has. What if she'd left a candle burning in there?"

"I should hope Fort wouldn't leave an open flame in her chambers," Kepler said dryly.

"She might, though. She's lost her keys twice since then. I think she's starting to be suspicious of why I keep "finding" them."

"You do skulk about often."

"I'm not skulking," Worry huffed. "If I can't study magic, the least I can do is study . . . everything else. And anyway, Fort made me the castle's caretaker. I take that seriously."

"A fair point," Kepler said, nodding his silvery head.

Gingerly, Worry stepped into the room, Kepler slipping in around her feet.

She stood in a dim office. Shelves of books filled one wall from floor to ceiling. A slight shudder, like a wave, went through their spines and a few floated off the shelves towards her.

"Legacy and Tradition: Respecting the Authority of One's Elders," was the title of the first.

"Er, no thank you," Worry said, gently nudging the book away. It floated back to its shelf with a slight air of misgiving.

Where would Fort have hidden an ancient, enchanted book? She bent down and reached her hands around Kepler.

"Can I pick you up?" she asked. The hair stood up on her arms as a chill went through her.

"I will float along, pretending you are carrying me," Kepler said.

With both hands, Worry held the weightless ghost cat up, pointing him towards various parts of the room, but the shifts in light were so subtle they were hard to interpret.

She turned to see that two of the books had been sneaking up on her.

"Openness and Transparency: The Case for Always Being Honest with Those Around Us," read the closest one.

"No, thank you," Worry said, hurrying through a doorway into the next room.

She passed a cozy sitting room with a large river rock fireplace and a mullioned window looking out over the dark, star-flecked ocean.

Beyond that was a small bathroom tiled with polished seashells, and after that a spartan bedroom.

Kepler's light illuminated a narrow bed in one corner, with a heavy trunk sitting at its feet. A threadbare wool rug muffled her steps. At a single narrow window was a slim gold telescope pointing horizontally out across the bay.

She thought she heard something and froze, tilting her head.

"Kepler," she whispered. "Did you hear that?"

He darted away through a wall and her chest clenched.

Seconds later, he returned. "No one's here. The hall is empty."

Her chest loosened a fraction.

She did a quick search of the room. There was nothing under the bed or under the rug. None of the stones were loose.

She approached the telescope. What had Fort been looking at? Bending slightly, careful not to bump the device, she peered through the eyepiece.

It took a few moments to get close enough that the image resolved into sharp focus. She sucked in a gasp. There was that many-spired castle she'd seen in the Tapestry of Travesties.

"Kepler, do you know what that place is?" she breathed. A shock of cold went through her face as Kepler joined her at the telescope, and she jerked back.

"Ow, jeez, I would have moved."

Kepler shrugged, his ruffle jiggling. "Efficiency. I figured we could both look just as easily."

She rubbed her face. "What is that place?"

"Some sharks have to keep swimming to breathe," he said heavily.

Her eyebrows lifted.

A bump from somewhere high above jolted her back to focus. Fort might return at any moment, and there was one place left to look.

She knelt in front of the trunk.

"Don't tell me you have that key, too," Kepler said.

"Of course not."

That didn't mean she didn't have options, though. Worry pulled out her lockpicks.

"You sure make a habit of learning disreputable things," Kepler said.

Worry frowned and her stomach churned. She didn't want to break into things. "This castle is full of ancient locks that Fort's lost the keys to. I wouldn't have been able to get into half the rooms without this."

Maybe Fort hadn't actually lost those keys, though. Maybe those were more secrets. Although, she didn't know why the room with all the chamber pots would have been some giant dark secret. Or the room full of canned asparagus.

And Fort did have a habit of losing things. Sometimes when people were so focused on giant, lofty challenges, they lost sight of the little everyday things, Worry reasoned.

The trunk clicked open with a burst of green fairy dust.

Inside were two tiny, very old blankets. Faded and worn. Each one had a name embroidered on it. The pink one read Hope, and the blue one read Worry. The lettering on Hope's was done in elegant gold loops. The 'W' on Worry's was also, but the tailor seemed to have run out of energy on the rest of the letters. They were done in a straightforward, businesslike script. Worry sighed.

Gently, Worry put them aside. Beneath that was a sketch-book. Worry flipped through it, recognizing Fort's handwriting on the labels. There were sketches of Worry and Hope, just doing everyday things. Farther back were rougher sketches of other people. A kind looking woman with a thick braid over one shoulder and a fluffy shawl read "Mistress Serenity". A tall, muscular man with a thick curly beard, many colorful tattoos, and a corduroy vest was labelled "Unity". Worry let out a long, sad breath. These must have been Fort's teachers. The last of the knights before her.

There were no other students.

With a pang of guilt for invading Fort's personal sketch-book, she put it aside.

Something clanked.

Frowning, she pushed aside another book, and a glint of metal caught her eye. A golden disk on a velvet chain. "For Bravery and Service to the Realm," Worry read aloud. Her eyes widened and she ran her fingers over the cool indentations. Fort had never mentioned winning a medal.

She flipped it over, but only a date was written on the back. Twenty years ago . . . Worry briefly counted on her fingers. Fort would have been around thirteen.

Gently, she set the medal aside. Below that was a sword. Its blade was dull and chipped, and its hilt was wrapped in worn, cracked leather.

She slid her fingers around it reverently, but then something below the sword caught her eye.

Her heart stopped.

Underneath was an ancient, leatherbound book. A glowing ribbon like woven seaweed made of light, was wrapped tightly around it, binding it closed, secured with a tiny shell clasp.

Forgetting the sword, she reached in and extracted it, running her fingers over the ancient cover. The golden letters reflected in the ghostly light. "Kepler."

"We found it, Kepler," she breathed.

68

Kepler started to say something about Narwhals, when a loud bang sounded from the entryway.

"Who's there?!" Fort shouted.

Worry hastily dumped everything but the book back into the trunk, shut it as quietly as she could, and dove under the bed. Kepler disappeared through a wall.

Fern zipped into the room, leaving a trail of sparkles as she shot to and fro.

Worry shrank back into the far corner as Fort's boots appeared.

She stopped in the middle of the rug. Green light tilted this way and that.

"I heard something," Fort said.

"I've checked everything. I didn't see anyone," Fern said, her voice high and sparkling.

Fort's boots moved away, towards the window, and Worry relaxed a fraction. Then Fort's hands appeared, bracing against the floor. She knelt down. There was only one thing to peer under in this room.

Worry grimaced, tensing, ready to explain, to be shouted at.

With a tiny pop, Fern appeared next to her. Without saying a word, or even looking at her, she tapped her wand. A thin, wavery veil surrounded her.

Worry's mouth dropped open, her whole body taut with tension, staring at Fern. *What is she doing?*

Fort's head appeared, and Fern lifted her wand higher, as if she'd come under the bed simply to illuminate the space.

69

Frowning, Fort moved this way and that, peering into all the corners, but her gaze slipped across Worry as if she wasn't there.

Worry's mind reeled. Fern was tricking her chosen knight. That wasn't supposed to be possible. Fairies chose their knights and then aided them, advised them. It was an ancient order that had always been this way.

Worry's stomach went cold, and she wanted to crawl out from under the bed, through that strange transparent veil, confess everything to Fort, and try to figure out what was going on together.

Fern still wasn't looking at her. *What are you doing?* Worry thought. *Why are you helping me?* Was she working with Kepler? *Am I doing something wrong?*

But Fort had told her there was no way to rescue Hope. And she'd been keeping things from her for years. Worry wanted to know the truth, and she wouldn't give her sister up for anything.

Even if it destroys the last of the Scholar Knights?

Worry pushed the thought aside. She had no reason to believe that would happen. Information couldn't hurt anyone, could it?

At last, Fort pushed up off the floor and collapsed onto the bed. It creaked and sagged under her weight.

"Guess I'm pretty jumpy tonight," Fort mumbled.

"Here, let me warm up your tea, and I'll get a fire going," Fern said gently. A moment later the room was warming and the smell of blueberry tea wafted in.

"Have you seen my notes? I can't find them anywhere."

"Oh yes, you left them in the hallway when you stopped to look at that painting."

"Ah, thank you," Fort stretched, stifling a yawn. "I'm so tired. But I should be doing more. I sent word out again though, sent out the call for every able-bodied fighter for thirty miles to get here as soon as possible. I tried to make it sound more urgent this time, but I still don't know if anyone will come." Her voice was tight, heavy and thick. The next words caught in her throat. "I lost her, Fern. I lost the last one. She was such a sweet girl. I hate to think—" Fort's voice cracked.

There was a long, heavy silence.

"There's one left," Fern said.

"Are you sure you haven't heard anything from Bluebell?"

Worry bit back a gasp. Who was Bluebell? The name felt like a warm bath, like perfect love and safety, like a cozy room on a stormy day.

"No, nothing," Fern said. "She's truly gone, it seems."

She's lying again, Worry thought immediately. She had no reason to think this, no evidence, but she felt in her gut it was true. *But why?*

"Well, you of anyone would know."

Fort slurped her tea and yawned heavily again.

"We've got . . . eighteen hours until the next one starts. I need to ready the rest of the defenses. Hopefully the others will be here by then. I'm just . . ." she yawned again. "I'm just going to take a quick . . . a quick . . ."

Fern caught the teacup neatly just before it hit the floor.

For the briefest moment, her eyes locked with Worry's.
She looked conflicted. Guilty?
She vanished in a cloud of green sparkles.

Using Gravity to Find the Invisible

How can we discover something we can't see? Gravity! That's how astronomers found the planet Neptune. Neptune is a gigantic planet for our solar system. It's 17 times the mass of the Earth! It's also extremely far away. (It's the farthest planet from the Sun, except for poor Pluto, who despite what scientists say will always be a planet in my heart.)

Astronomers and mathematicians were observing nearby Uranus, when they noticed a slight wobble in Uranus' movement. They realized that there must be some giant object passing nearby, like a giant magnet passing near a metal ball, pulling it towards it just slightly.

They used math to calculate where this secret massive planet might be hiding. They pointed their telescopes in that direction, and they found it! That must have been an amazing moment. I bet they felt like geniuses.

Let's practice finding invisible objects! Gravity is a lot like magnetism in many ways, except that magnetism is much, much stronger. So, we'll use magnets in this activity to represent gravity.

Get some magnets (4 or 5) and a piece of stiff paper or thin cardboard. Place the magnets on the ground, spaced apart, and balance the paper over them. Try to keep the paper flat.

(So, you're using the magnets kind of like table legs.)

Now take a metal ball or marble and roll it across the paper. Try to roll it so that it passes near a magnet by not quite directly over it. Notice how the magnets affect the motion of the metal ball. This is just like how strong gravitational forces would affect a mass travelling nearby.

For one other cool solar-system activity, check out "If the Moon Were Only One Pixel: A Tediously Accurate Scale Model of the Solar System." https://joshworth.com/dev/pixel space/pixelspace_solarsystem.html

Chapter Nine:
Tides

WORRY winced as Fort gave a loud snort and rolled over. The bed creaked and groaned.

It had better not break.

Worry weighed her choices. If she snuck out, and Fort woke up and saw her . . . She shook her head. She couldn't afford to wait until Fort left.

Tucking the book into her bag, Worry squirmed her way out from under the bed. Keeping flat to the floor, she crept across the spare wool rug.

Fort grunted and mumbled something.

Worry froze, staring at her. Fort had bundled up her blankets and was clutching them to her chest, curling her body around them. Her eyes twitched under her lids. "No," she said. "Eggs."

That sure was a stressful-sounding dream to be having about breakfast. A pang of sympathy hit her. Fort tried so hard at everything. And her own fairy godmother was lying to her!

What must it be like for Fort, being the only Scholar Knight? Hope felt so much pressure, being the only student here. And she had Worry for company and sympathy. Fort was the only Scholar and had been the only student in her day, too. Was it nice to have had all those teachers, or did that make the pressure even worse? And then, to have the teachers pass on one at a time, leaving Fort completely alone in this castle for years. Well, except for Fern, of course. No wonder Fort refused to tell Worry anything. She must feel like she had to do it all on her own.

Don't worry, she thought. *You're not the only one trying. I'll fix this.*

Even as she thought it, it felt a bit silly to think that she could do what Fort—smart, powerful, unstoppably hard-working Fort—couldn't.

Worry slipped out of Fort's chambers with a massive sigh of relief and broke into a run. She sprinted for the nearest exit and pushed her way out into the salty night air. Kepler reappeared at her side as she descended the steps two or three at a time.

"What happened?" Kepler asked.

"Fern hid me!"

"Fern? No. But . . . was it a trick?"

"Only on Fort," Worry said, out of breath. She sure was doing a lot more running than usual. *I should have thought of practicing this.* Having keys was good but running up and down staircases all night was a type of practice that hadn't occurred to her.

She spilled out onto the beach and skidded to a stop in the rocky sand.

Pulling out her own tiny telescope, she scanned the island on the other side of the bay. A tiny bit of reflected moonlight caught her eye.

There. The outline of a spire.

There must be a reason Fort had been watching that castle, and a reason the Tapestry of Travesties had shown it to her. She'd just better be careful not to fall in that bottomless chasm.

A vast expanse of water stretched between her and the island, but the tide was receding.

"What's the plan?" Kepler asked.

"Well, I could look for a boat, or try to make one, but . . . I think the tide's on its way out, and I have a feeling that we might be able to reach the other castle at low tide. If it's low enough. Do you know how long it takes for the tide to go out?"

Kepler only stared at her; his lips clamped tight.

"Fair enough," she said. "I wouldn't have thought tides had anything to do with astronomy, though." She interlaced her fingers behind her head and stared at the lapping waves. "Maybe I'll give it a minute, see if the tide looks like it's going out far enough. I'll read your book in meantime." Kepler's ears perked up and he ran three quick circles around her.

"Will you keep watch for Fort?" she asked.

Kepler spun around, his tail flying out. "Yes! I'll let you know if she's coming. Don't leave without me!"

"Of course not!"

He sprinted back up the stairs, and Worry sat on the bottom step, pulling out Kepler's book. A cloud of fireflies drifted over, hovering around her shoulders and illuminating the pages.

"Thank you," she whispered, running a hand across the leather cover, putting a fingertip on the cool seaweed that bound it. Would opening it break the enchantment on Kepler?

Gently, she tried the shell clasp, and it clicked open. Unwinding the seaweed, its glow fading, she waited for Kepler to return, excited, but nothing happened. She shrugged and opened the first page. Enchantments could be tough to break.

Words and diagrams and lengthy equations appeared on the pages as she turned them. Unlike in Aristotle's book, the last page had no disembodied writer to talk to, only a sketch of a cat with a pointed moustache.

She returned to the first page and began to read.

There were long lists of numbers, observations that Aristotle would have approved of, and tables of data. Sketches of the sky with unfamiliar planets labelled in their positions.

To her excitement, there was a whole section on tides.

"There are two tides per day," Worry read aloud. "I believe they are caused by the moon, but I don't know how, only that that seems to be the case. It is some harmony I don't understand."

How the Force of Gravity Causes the Tides

The force of gravity is weakest on the far side.

Force of gravity

The moon attracts the water.

The pull of the moon's gravity is strongest on the closest side.

The earth is also pulled toward the moon, but it moves less than the water.

Low tides where the water recides.

"Caused by the moon!" Worry exclaimed. How did that work? "In a twenty-four-hour day—oh, that's the same as here, I wonder if the tides work the same, too—that would mean twelve hours per tide, or around six hours in and six hours out."

She lifted her gaze to the moonlit sand. A crab scuttled across the silvery surface and disappeared into a hole. The bay was a long expanse of exposed sand, littered with clumps of seaweed. The island poked up out of the water about a mile away, its base rocky and exposed, its top spiky with evergreens.

"Okay, it was high tide right before the syzygy, so I probably have an hour or two until the tide's at its lowest point. Does the tide always go out the same distance, though?" She tried to remember how far the water usually went out, wishing she'd paid more attention.

She flipped another page. Kepler's world had only one moon, it seemed. How strange! If they only had one moon, then why were there two tides per day? And would the tides in her world work the same as in his? She stared up at the moons. Only the red moon moved around the planet. The other two were fixed. So maybe only the moving moon caused the pattern of tides? But how could that be? Did the shape of the beach matter?

She struggled to keep it all in her mind. Three moons, one moving. A high tide around every twelve hours. A regular rhythm, but with varying depths.

She understood now why Kepler had been so annoyed when Aristotle said the tides were caused by the wind. But she also understood why it had been so hard for people to figure out.

She looked again across the bay at the tiny island that was her goal. Only a small amount of water remained between it and her.

Science Activity:

Sometimes in science, we know why something happens, but other times we only know that it does. This was the case for Kepler. He had a large amount of data from Tycho Brahe about how the moon and planets moved, and he used it to figure out that the planets moved in elliptical orbits, and he was sure the moon caused the tides, but he didn't know how that was happening. Still, having good data and noticing some patterns are a good first step on the road to understanding.

In this activity, let's take some data of our own, and we'll see why it was so tough to understand the tides.

Choose a location that is near the ocean. It can be near where you live, if you have tides, but you could also pick a place you'd like to go to, or a place you saw in a movie. I'll use Langley, on Whidbey Island.

Next, get yourself a notepad to take some data! Each day for a full week, record the times of the high tides at your location and the times when the moon is highest in the sky. You can also draw a picture of the moon to depict whether it's full, half, quarter, etc. For your notes on the moon, you can either observe directly, or you can use the SkyView app to follow its path, or the Sky and Telescope _Interactive Sky Chart_. Just input the day, time, and zip code of your chosen location.

For the tides, you can observe them directly or you can use the _US Harbors Tide Charts_.

After you've taken all your data, what do you notice? Do the tides correspond to the position of the moon in a regular way? What might be affecting this?

You might notice a pattern, but you might not. It turns out that even though the moon causes the tides, they vary a lot because they're also affected by the shape of the coastline, the gravity of the sun, and the rotation of the Earth! This is part of why figuring out how the world works can be so tough. There are so many things that all have an effect. We'll learn more about this in later chapters.

Chapter Ten:
Pendulums

A YOWLING like a siren reached her ears. Kepler shot around the base of the castle, pelting towards her.

"Time to go!" he shouted.

She slammed the book closed and hastily stuffed it into her bag.

"What's—"

"No time, no time, let's go!" he shouted, whizzing past her in a blur of light.

She leapt to her feet and took off after him, her bag banging against her side and her boots splashing through puddles.

"What's going on, Kepler?" she yelled, gaining on the ghost.

"Fort figured out you took—you were in her quarters."

Worry craned her head to look behind her, stumbling over the uneven ground, to see if Fort was running after them. "Is she—"

"Nope, nope. She's got reinforcements now."

"Soldiers?"

"Volunteers. From the neighboring villages."

"Ah, well, great."

"Yes, except they're after you now. I told them I'd seen you down in the library, but that won't slow them down for long." He gave a frustrated growl. "I really wish I could do things sometimes. Like close doors. And turn locks, for instance."

Worry pumped her arms, her pounding feet splattering mud. It soaked her pant legs but sailed right through Kepler.

"Anything else I should know?" Worry asked.

"An octopus can change color and texture to blend in with its surroundings!" he shouted.

"That sure would be handy!"

"Yes," Kepler said.

They were about halfway across the muddy bay, and Worry's boots were sinking inches deep with every step in the thick mud, when a distant shout reached her ears.

Against her better judgement, she turned briefly to see a group of adults emerging from the castle, shouting and pointing at her.

They took off at a run towards her. They looked like they might have practiced running a time or two more than she had.

She yelped and picked up the pace, slipped on a clump of seaweed, and splashed into a puddle. Flailing, with the incorporeal Kepler trying to help her up and succeeding only in sending chills through her, she pushed herself back up. *Okay, Worry*, she thought, *just run as fast as you can without falling.*

She fell a few more times before she reached a narrow channel of black water flowing between her and the island. She barely paused at the edge before wading in, holding her satchel over her head. "Please don't be deep," she muttered.

The icy water rose to her chest, and she felt like she'd been fully submerged in a giant Kepler. Kepler floated across the surface, urging her to hurry.

The frozen current tugged at her, and she pushed her legs forward, nearly losing her footing on the sand that gave way beneath her feet.

Finally, the far bank appeared, the water became gradually shallower, and at last she emerged, dripping and shivering, on the far side.

She didn't stop, just struggled in her wet clothes to the rocky base of the island.

A narrow set of stone steps wound up through smooth, red-barked madrona trees, their wide yellow leaves littering the ground.

Worry was grateful for the climb, even though her leg muscles burned in protest and her wet pants chafed, because it warmed her slightly.

The air around her lightened and the sky overhead became a paler shade of gray as the sun began to rise. Far below, their pursuers were gaining. She was only halfway up the dizzying steps when they crossed the channel and started up after her.

She swallowed hard and pushed herself to climb faster, grabbing tree branches to haul herself up the steep steps.

84

At last, she stumbled onto the top: a bare promontory of black volcanic rock and sparse yellow grass. There, only feet away, was the chasm she'd seen in the Tapestry of Travesties.

The chasm was a sudden gash in the black rock, as if the island had split in half. On the other side of the chasm rose the many-spired castle. Its lean was even more pronounced up close. The central tower tilted at almost a forty-five-degree angle to one side. The other spires were straighter but leaned at their own crazy angles in all directions.

She could also now see that it was covered in silver symbols. Planets, moons, comets, mathematical equations. Large balconies extended on all sides, each with its own large telescope, pointed at the heavens.

A thick metal cable overhead ran from one side of the chasm to the other, and from this cable three pendulums hung, each a different size and shape, and each its own length. They swung towards her and away, each with its own rhythm and speed. Her stomach gave a swoop as she watched, imagining trying to jump from one to the next.

She approached hesitantly, knowing the villagers would be there any minute, and peered down into it. A cold wind, like damp breath hit her face. The sun wasn't high enough to send light far down into it, so she could only see a few feet.

"Hurry," Kepler said. "We've got to get across."

He skittered over to the edge and peered back down the steps. "They're a lot better at stair climbing," he said, sounding both panicked and impressed. "You've got maybe a minute."

85

Her heart thundered, remembering the little image of herself from the tapestry, falling into the chasm.

She gulped, picked up a rock and dropped it in, just to see. Maybe it wasn't that deep.

She listened, and for a long while she heard it falling. Slowly, the sound faded, but she never heard it hit the bottom. She dropped a few more in, just in case she'd missed the sound of the impact.

Nothing.

A horrified groan escaped her lips.

"Come on, come on," Kepler said.

"Hang on," Worry said, noticing a plaque and a set of gears at the edge.

"Thirty seconds," Kepler said.

"If I don't take my time to figure this out, there's no point anyway," she said.

The plaque had an image of her planet, with a little "you are here" arrow indicating that she stood at the edge of a pit that ran the full diameter of the planet. She frowned. It looked like the chasm went all the way through the center of the planet and out the other side. That wasn't possible, was it?

She thought of Aristotle and his idea that earth and water wanted to be as far down as possible. What would happen in a pit like this? Would they fall to the center of the planet and then stop, stuck there?

That didn't make sense, because she knew that when she dropped something it fell faster and faster. So, when it got to the center, it must be going really fast.

But when you crossed the center of the planet, you'd be going upwards again. That didn't make sense at all. She picked up another stone and tossed it into the air. It rose a few feet, slowed down, paused, then fell back down. Would that happen in the tunnel? Would she fall through to the other side of the planet?

She didn't have time to think about this, she had to get across, so she turned to the panel. Three levers and three cranks were lined up in two rows.

Randomly, she pulled the first lever. A brake was applied, and the first pendulum ground to a stop, hanging straight down. She pulled the second and third, and those pendulums stopped as well. Well, it was nice that at least they weren't moving anymore. But the first was too far away. She knew she couldn't jump that far, and even if she could, she couldn't get to the second, let alone the third.

She started them swinging again. The first pendulum came close enough to the edge that she could have jumped to it, but it was out of sync with the next pendulum.

I see. I have to adjust them so that the second pendulum is closest to me when the first pendulum is farthest away, so that they're close enough to jump between them.

"Back away from the machine, Worry," a deep voice rang out.

She spun around and saw the last of the five adults climb over the edge. They were a motley group, with patched clothing and battered swords, but they were each several feet taller than she was and looked barely winded from their long climb. Worry didn't understand how that could be possible.

Faint early morning light shone in their eyes. She raised her palms in a placating gesture. "Please, I'm just trying to help," she said.

"Fort said as much, but you're to come with us," the leader said. He took a step closer.

"Please," she said again. "Please, I need to get Hope back."

"We know you want her back, but that's impossible. The best thing you can do now is not make any more trouble for Fort. She sent us to get you, when we should be back defending the castle for . . . what might be coming."

The others were nodding. "You're wasting valuable resources, kid."

Worry swallowed. There might be truth to what they were saying. Yes, she was trying to help, but she didn't know what was going on. Because Fort refused to tell her.

"Look," Worry said. "That totally makes sense, and I want to go back and help, but I can't do that unless Fort will be honest with me."

"You're just a kid," he said.

Her throat tightened and tears rose in her eyes. "Maybe, but I still have to do something. I can't sit around hiding, not knowing what's happening."

"That's a mistake," he said. "You're making things worse."

"You've already made things worse, by opening the tower," another added.

Worry scanned their faces and saw only earnestness. She swallowed hard and shook her head, looking down. Who was she to be trying to fix things? She was just making a mess of everything.

Out of the corner of her eye, she saw something strange. There, in the chasm, a rock appeared, floating, for a second, before falling back down. She blinked, her vision swimming with tears.

Another rock appeared, rising from the depths, pausing, and then falling back down. *What?* They were familiar rocks. They were the ones she'd dropped. She thought of Aristotle, of her own ideas about what would happen with a tunnel that went all the way through the planet.

A very, very risky idea occurred to her.

A thousand objections immediately suggested themselves.

The villagers were edging closer, raising their hands. One carried a length of rope looped across her chest. If they caught her, they'd bring her back to the castle and lock her up.

"Please, I just need to get my sister back. I just need to help."

"We can't promise that, kid."

Desperately, she scanned the narrow promontory on which she stood. All sides were steep cliffs. There were only the stairs in front of her—with the grownups in her way—and the chasm at her back. No other ways off this ledge.

She took half a step back, and the leader lunged for her.

A yowling, white blur shot in between them, colliding straight with his face.

"Ah!" he shrieked, pawing at his face, waving his arms and shaking his head as if trying to wave off a mosquito. "Cold!" he shrieked. The others dove in to help. Kepler leapt between them, like a surprise internal ice bath. She had only a second to make up her mind.

Clenching her fists, she stepped backwards off the edge of the chasm.

Safety Notes:

Don't try this at home! Worry's planet is special. It's smaller than Earth, so it has less gravity, and it has a tunnel going perfectly through its center. Will she be okay? What will happen as she falls through the chasm? To understand that, we'll need to understand some things about gravity!

In the last activity, we saw how hard it can be to understand the world, because there are so many complex factors that go into each phenomenon. How can we fix this? One way is to ask ourselves a simpler question. Simplify or slow down the thing we're looking at, to try to understand it better, and to try to rule out some of the many complicated factors. Many scientists and mathematicians use this trick to solve complex problems. I love using this trick when I'm solving puzzles!

So, what's a simpler gravity situation? Pendulums! Legend has it that Galileo Galilei was staring at a chandelier swinging back and forth in Pisa Cathedral when he realized he could use its motion to understand something about gravity. What causes a pendulum to swing? Gravity!

Pendulums Activity:

In this activity, let's figure out what affects the speed of a pendulum. All you need is a stopwatch, and a weight tied to a string. A necklace with a pendant works great. To start, hold the necklace by one end with the weight dangling down. Grab the weight and lift it up and to the side a bit, keeping the string taut. Have someone start the stopwatch at the same time as you let go of the pendulum. Watch the pendulum swing down and back. Keep your hand holding it as still as possible. Stop the stopwatch right as soon as it comes back to its starting point. The amount of time this takes is called the period of the pendulum. (You could also let the pendulum swing 3 times and then divide the time you get by 3, sometimes this helps with accuracy.)

What do you think might affect the time this takes?
Would the weight affect it?

Try adding more weight to your pendulum (maybe add another pendant to your necklace.) Make sure you keep the starting point of the pendulum and the length of the string the exact same! (When we're experimenting, it's important to only change one thing at a time so we know what causes what.) You might want to make a little table in your notebook to record the weight of your pendulum and the period of the swing so you can see if there are any patterns.

Next, let's see if length of the string affects it! This time, keep the weight exactly the same, but repeat your measurement of the period with different lengths of the string. Does the period change?

You could also try playing around with the *Phet Pendulum Lab*. Try changing the string lengths and the weights and see what changes the time it takes to swing back and forth.

Bonus challenge question: Does the starting height of the pendulum change its period?

Results: Making precises measurements is tough, but what you should notice is that the mass doesn't affect the time the pendulum takes to swing back and forth. This directly contradicts Aristotle! Why? Because it means that different weights are falling at exactly the same speed. Aristotle thought that heavier objects would fall faster, but Galileo showed with his pendulums that they don't! The surprising fact about pendulums is that it doesn't matter how heavy the weight is, or how high you start the swing from (as long as it's not a super big angle). There are only two things that affect the speed and period of the pendulum: 1. The length of the string and 2. The strength of gravity.

One super cool fact: you can use pendulums to measure how strong gravity is. If you were suddenly teleported to a random planet, and you didn't know which one, you could use a pendulum to precisely measure the strength of gravity, which you could use to figure out which planet you were on! (Assuming you were somewhere in the solar system and had a table of the gravitational strengths of the different planets...)

Chapter Eleven:
The Bottomless Pit

WORRY screamed as she plunged into darkness, the dank air whistling in her ears as she fell, as if into the throat of some enormous, subterranean dragon.

She screamed until she ran out of breath, then sucked in more of the dank air and screamed some more, all the while falling faster and faster.

Eventually, when nothing horrible had happened, she stopped screaming.

The wind rose and rose, plastering her hair straight up; her braid was like a lifted tail. She squinted against the blackness, but there was nothing.

At any moment, she expected to careen into something. The side of the chasm, some ill-placed ledge. Maybe a giant tongue would lick out and scoop her into the mouth of some invisible monster.

She screamed again, thinking of the monster and what it might feel like to be chewed up. But, when that didn't happen, and she continued to plummet without incident, she stopped.

It was surprising how quickly one got used to speeding through the center of a planet at speeds faster than one thought possible.

By waving her arms, she could change her position. It was like swimming, and she realized she could change her speed. Feet first was fastest. Belly first, with her arms and legs spread wide, was the slowest. She'd never noticed before how powerful air could be! It was so light, barely noticeable usually, but at high speeds, it really made a difference! What if there were no air here? Had Aristotle missed the effects of air, too?

Eventually, she realized she was slowing down.

I think I've passed through the center of the planet. Was she now blasting up towards the other side?

This seemed to be the case. Slower and slower she went. She whizzed past colorful, flickering lights, too quickly to make out their shapes.

Light dawned up ahead. She sped towards the brightness, the spot growing larger and larger. The closer she got, the slower she fell. Could it even really be called falling anymore? Or was she now flying?

Through the hole above, she began to see trees, fireflies, more flickers of colorful lights. Slower and slower she went, at last just barely popping through the hole, rising like a whale lifting out of the ocean in a graceful leap.

She had a quick glimpse of evening light. Orange rays slanting through campfires. Great trailing moss hanging like shawls from ancient trees. Everywhere, around the campfires, lounging in trees, fluttering over the hole, were delicate gossamer fairies.

Lilting music cut out as she rose into their midst. They stared openmouthed at her. She gave the tiniest of waves as she paused, then, with a swoop of her stomach, began to fall back into the hole.

A few of the fairies whizzed after her, but she was quickly gaining speed, and they couldn't catch her. For a while she went back to screaming.

She felt it this time, that moment she passed through the center of the planet. That moment when she was no longer speeding up but just for the briefest of moments there was that same weightless sensation she'd had at the top of the Astronomy Tower. And then she was gradually slowing again.

As she approached the opening she'd originally started at, she scanned the bright spot for something to grab onto. She definitely didn't want to risk another fall through the center of the planet.

She reached her arms up and prepared to grab whatever appeared.

She lifted gently above the hole, to almost the height she'd started at, extended her foot, and stepped back onto the ledge she'd leapt off several minutes earlier.

She grinned, full of exhilaration and triumph. The others were gone.

Her stomach went ice-cold as a ball of light collided with her. It roiled through her shoulders, neck, out one arm, then back to her stomach again.

"Ow, Kepler, eesh!" She dodged out of his way.

Silvery tears were dripping from his pointed moustache. He wiped them away with his tiny paws and stared mournfully up at her.

"I watched you disappear," he said quietly.

She knelt and ran her hands over his back. "I'm so sorry to worry you, Kepler. I'm fine. I dropped some rocks in earlier and they came back. I thought I could trick them into leaving."

His eyes widened. "That was incredibly . . ."

She expected him to say something like 'brilliant' or 'brave.'

". . . dangerous."

"Oh. Yes." That, too. "I had to, though."

He let out a long sigh and crouched lower. "Well, it sure worked. They watched the hole for a while, then your screaming cut out and . . . they felt awful. They're on their way to let Fort know."

Worry's stomach twisted. Fort was going to feel horrible, too. Worry didn't want to add to Fort's burdens. *I have to keep going, though.*

"Are you okay?" Worry asked Kepler.

He sat daintily. "Oh, yes. I'm all right, thank you."

She let out a long sigh. There was a ringing in her ears from the wind, and her stomach was still adjusting to being stationary.

She turned and stared up at the castle, silhouetted with early morning sunlight.

It was time to cross the chasm.

Who hasn't tried to dig a tunnel to the other side of the Earth? Could you actually make a tunnel through the center of a planet? This is such a fun thought experiment! The first answer is probably not on Earth, but possibly on Worry's planet, which is much smaller. The centers of planets get incredibly hot because of the weight of all the rock and dirt and oceans pressing down on them. The temperature at the center of the Earth can get up to around 10,000 degrees Fahrenheit. Iron melts at only 2,800 degrees, steel melts at 2,500 degrees. Wood burns at only 400 degrees. So, all our tools that we might use to dig or reinforce the tunnel would be destroyed. Not only that, but the pressure at the center of the Earth is 3.6 million atmospheres, which means it's 3.6 million times the pressure that we feel. (Have you heard that diamonds are made by squishing carbon? Well, that only takes about 60,000 atmospheres of pressure.) But Worry's planet is much smaller, and it doesn't have a liquid core, like our Earth does. (Side note, did you know that the Earth used to be solid rock? It didn't use to have a liquid core, but eventually over time, as the weight of the planet compressed itself inward, its core melted. This is called the "Iron Catastrophe"! You can read more about all this fascinating stuff in the *National Geographic Education article entitled "Core"*. But back to Worry's planet. Her planet is still solid rock, so it might be more doable. If you could dig this tunnel, then what Worry experiences in the story is exactly what would happen. As you fell down the tunnel, you'd go faster and faster. The air would get hotter, too, from the increased pressure. Your ears might pop just like when you swim deeper underwater (the atmosphere is like a liquid, too, it's thinner and lighter than water, but still very heavy! We just don't notice it because we're used to it.) One of the weirdest things about going through the tunnel is that the force of gravity gets less and less as you go down. The math of this is a little complex, but basically, only the mass that's below you affects you. The stuff that's above you gets balanced out. So, as you fall, it's like you're standing on a tinier and tinier planet. You're still speeding up, but not speeding up as much as you were initially. (You would also probably hit what we call "terminal velocity" which is where you're not speeding up anymore because the force of the air pushing on you is balancing out the gravity pulling on you. So, you end up going at a constant speed.) In the very center of the planet, if you could stop yourself there, you would find yourself in a cavern where you were completely weightless. Just floating around as if you were in a spaceship! But it would be hard to stop there, because you'd be going incredibly fast at that point! In fact, you'd shoot right through the center of the planet as if you were fired from a rocket. As long as you didn't hit the walls of the tunnel, you'd head straight up to the surface on the far side! If there were no air resistance at all, and if the planet were perfectly circular, you'd rise just above the planet's surface on the other side, just like a ball thrown into the air pauses for a moment at its peak, and then you'd fall straight back through. You'd arrive at exactly the spot you left! As long as you never hit the walls or slowed yourself down in any way, you could bounce back and forth like this forever! It would take you exactly the same amount of time every time you bounced back and forth. In fact, you could even set your watch by it or build a clock that used this to measure the time, just like grandfather clocks use pendulums to measure the time.

Story Prompt: Could you imagine a planet with a tunnel like this, or maybe many tunnels? What would people use them for? Brainstorm, outline, or write a short story about someone living on a planet like this. Are they human, or some other kind of creature? Is there air on their planet?

Chapter Twelve:
The Leaning Castle

WORRY cracked her knuckles and approached the chasm again. What if she jumped in again? Could she fall through and pop back up on the other edge of the chasm? Too risky. It was such a long distance through the center of the planet that the tiniest amount of speed to the side might cause her to hit the edge of the tunnel.

She examined the panel with its three levers and three cranks. Flipping each lever to the 'off' position, she stopped the pendulums from swinging. Then she spun the cranks. These cranks changed the lengths of the pendulums.

If I make them as different as possible, their differences will be more extreme, and I can see what happens. She made one as short as possible, one as long as possible, and left the third where it was.

When the pendulums were swinging, she immediately saw that the shorter string made the pendulum swing back and forth faster. The longest string took the longest amount of time.

All those pendulums look different. Doesn't it matter that one is heavier?

She reset them all to the same length and started them moving. They all swung at exactly the same speed now.

How strange. The weight doesn't seem to matter. That's not what Aristotle would have expected.

An idea hit her. Keeping them all the same length, she started the pendulums swinging one at a time, so that when the first was as far away as possible, the second was as close as possible, so that they nearly touched. Then, when the second was as far as possible, the third was as close as possible, and those two touched. Because they were all going at exactly the same speed, they kept up this regular pattern.

"Impressive," Kepler said.

"Well, I had a lot of time to think. While I was in the bottomless pit of despair."

"I suppose bottomless pits of despair are good for that," Kepler said.

Clenching her fists, she hopped onto the first pendulum, moving with it as it swung. Landing on it changed its swing a tiny amount, but it was a lot heavier than she was, and it didn't change much. She easily leapt to the second pendulum, and then the third.

With a triumphant yell, she landed on the other side.

Spinning around to see if Kepler had made it, she watched him hop up to the cable that crossed the chasm and trot calmly across it.

He leapt gracefully down to join her and sat licking his paw with a slightly smug expression.

She pouted. "Had you thought of that the whole time?"

"Yes."

"Why didn't you say anything?"

"You looked like you were having fun."

She opened her mouth to protest, then laughed. "Okay, yeah, that was pretty fun."

Together they climbed the marble steps to the foot of the leaning castle. Above an enormous door were engraved the words "Philosophy is written in this grand book, the universe, which stands continually open to our gaze."

How beautiful, she thought. There was so much to see and understand in the world. So much that we took for granted every day.

Below that, a second line read "It is written in the language of mathematics, and its characters are triangles, circles, and other geometric figures . . ."

She thought of how she'd used her knowledge of circles to find Kepler's book, and how within that book she'd learned that the moons travelled in ellipses around her planet. Math was sometimes hard, but, like learning another language might let her speak to people from other kingdoms, in a way, math let her speak to the universe. The hair on her arms stood on end, and she shivered.

As she stood transfixed on the threshold, marveling at the beauty of the world, the door was thrown open. A boy about her age stood staring at her.

He wasn't quite solid, but he wasn't fully transparent like Kepler. He looked mostly like a boy, but with the occasional shimmer, and she could just make out the far wall through him. He wore elegant purple robes and a jaunty purple hat.

He glanced down at her cat. "Hello, Kepler," he said. "It's been a while!"

"Narwhals have a tusk that is actually an elongated tooth," Kepler said.

"Ah, right. Still enchanted, my friend? Sorry, buddy."

"You know Kepler?" Worry blurted out.

The boy smiled widely at her. "Hello, my name is Galileo." He placed a hand flat on his chest and gave an elegant bow. His hat fell off.

"Oh. Hi. My name's Worry."

He snatched his hat back up and thrust it onto his head, looking at her curiously. "Really?"

"Oh. Yeah."

"It's not a nickname?"

"Unfortunately, not."

"That must be rough."

"It's not my favorite, no."

Galileo nodded sympathetically.

"Sorry, are you an astronomer, too?" she asked.

"Oh, yes, I am!"

"And you're not enchanted?"

He glanced around at his tilted castle. "I mean, I'm sort of under house arrest here. Like I was towards the end of my actual life on Earth." He sighed. "But no. Not enchanted."

"You look too young to have been arrested," Worry said.

"Oh, I just prefer this. Just like Kepler prefers being a cat. Reminds me to stay curious. Would you like to come in?"

"Yes, thank you," Worry said. "I'm wondering if you can help me with something, actually."

He led her into the castle, which was lit by chandeliers swinging to and fro in a way that was slightly dizzying. She quickly told him the story of the tower and Hope, and Kepler's enchantment.

"You reopened the tower?" Galileo said, his voice rising with excitement. "That's wonderful!"

Her stomach churned. "I'm not so sure. Do you know what happened to it? Why they sealed it off? Why the astronomers are all gone and almost all the Scholar Knights are, too?"

"No. All I know is that they built it to reach the red moon. Telescopes work better when you bring them up high. There's less air between you and the stars, so things are clearer."

"Did they ever actually reach the red moon?" Worry asked breathlessly.

"I don't know. They mostly asked me about my telescopes, and what I knew about gravity."

Worry's heart caught in her throat. "Do you have a telescope I could use to see the red moon?"

"Yes, I have several."

Her heart flipped over. "Can we go look?"

"Well, the red moon is below the horizon now. It will rise later tonight. We can look then, if you'd like."

"Yes! Please. Thank you!"

104

"My pleasure! I make all my telescopes myself. I even grind the lenses myself. Or I did. When I could touch things." He waved a transparent hand through a nearby lamp sadly. "The astronomers and I were actually working on turning this whole castle into a giant telescope. Maybe you could help me polish the lenses?"

"Of course," Worry said. "I'd be happy to."

He grinned and ran up a spiraling staircase, motioning for her to follow. She pounded after him, thinking ruefully that yet again she found herself sprinting headlong up a staircase. Kepler silently followed.

At the top of the tower was a giant circular window. It was made of glass around two feet thick at the edges and four feet thick in the middle. Through it, Worry could see the blue sky, distorted by the lens's shape. Galileo pointed to a pile of cloths.

"The astronomers were here working on it a while ago. I guess it's been decades now. I kept hoping they'd come back. It's incredibly frustrating to be a ghost and not be able to make anything anymore."

"I can imagine," Worry said, picking up a cloth and gently polishing the enormous lens. She felt like she was standing inside a giant eyeball, looking out. "You don't happen to know how to break Kepler's enchantment, do you?" she asked.

"I don't, sorry," he said.

"But you knew him? Here?" she asked.

"On Earth. We were scientists at the same time. He had very good ideas. We both disagreed with Aristotle, which was a very unpopular opinion at the time."

Worry scrubbed a little harder at a speck of dirt on the lens. "He seemed very wise," she said.

"Brilliant, absolutely brilliant," Galileo said, fiddling with his brooch. "But he missed some things."

"Like what?"

"Well, he thought heavier things fall faster."

"They don't?"

Galileo grinned and motioned for her to follow him to an open window. They were at the top of the leaning tower. Looking out, she could see the ground far below. She really hoped this tower would stay up.

Two ornate vases, one large and green and one tiny and yellow, were perched on the windowsill.

"Push them over the edge," Galileo said.

Worry did a double take. "Are you sure?"

He nodded.

Checking to make sure nothing was below, she pushed the two of them off. They plummeted to the ground, shattering at exactly the same moment.

Almost as soon as they had shattered, they reappeared, whole, on the windowsill. Her eyebrows lifted.

Kepler hopped up, his tail twitching in anticipation, and batted a paw at the vases. His paw went right through, and he meowed plaintively at Worry. She obediently pushed the vases off again. Seeing them hit the ground at exactly the same time again, despite their sizes, she frowned at them.

"But Aristotle said—"

"He didn't realize that air was messing up his results," Galileo said. "Lighter things like feathers are more affected by the air, so they fall slower. But if there was no air, everything would fall at precisely the same speed."

"That's so weird," Worry said. "How did you figure that out?"

He pointed to one of the swinging chandeliers. "Pendulums! I noticed that the mass of a pendulum doesn't affect how fast it goes. Understanding gravity is hard, because things fall so quickly. It's hard to figure out what's going on. Pendulums, and rolling things down gradual inclines, slowed things down enough for me to figure things out."

"That's so clever," she said, and he smiled. "So . . . what about . . ." she hesitated. This was the question she was most afraid to ask. Was Hope just destined to be somewhere else? "Aristotle said that earth and water both moved down, and air and fire naturally move up. That . . . things all have their own natural places?"

"A pretty idea, but wrong," Galileo said with confidence. A great weight lifted off her heart. As if its natural state was not in fact to weigh her down. "No, Aristotle thought the Earth was the center of the universe and surrounded by crystalline spheres. And that everything had its own natural place. And that the stars and planets moved in spheres. Which is all incorrect. He really loved spheres. I see why. They're very nice shapes."

"True, yes," Worry said, moving back to the great lens and resuming her polishing.

Galileo's voice rose in excitement. "But you have to go with the evidence! And from all my observations, all the evidence was pointing towards Copernicus's idea that the sun was in fact the center, and the Earth and other planets moved around the sun."

"Fascinating," Worry said, trying to picture this.

Kepler gave a mournful yowl and put his head in his paws.

"They move in ellipses, as my friend here discovered."

Kepler looked slightly more cheerful.

"And faster when they get closer to the sun, and slower when they get farther away."

"So even planets speed up and slow down?" Worry asked, amazed.

"Yes!"

"Why don't we feel that?"

Galileo opened his mouth and closed it again. "Huh. You know, that's an interesting question."

Her stomach warmed. Fort's response to Worry's questions was usually to tell her not to ask them. Or that her questions would bring destruction to the world. This was definitely nicer.

"Anyway," Galileo said. "People did NOT like me saying Aristotle was wrong. No, they did not. The Roman Inquisition put me under house arrest for the last years of my life."

"I'm sorry. What's the—"

"But I kept learning! And writing! I found that the distance travelled by a falling object is proportional to the square of the time it has fallen! Hah! Take that, Aristotle!" He punched the air.

"Er, yes. Bet that made him feel pretty silly," Worry said, having no idea what any of that meant.

Galileo looked at her. "Oh. Sorry. What I mean is, let's say an object falls one foot in a certain amount of time. It's speeding up that whole time, so it's falling faster and faster. When it's fallen for twice as long, it will have fallen four feet. When it's fallen for three times as long, it will have fallen nine feet. Four times as long, sixteen feet, and so on."

"I see. By 'square' you mean you're multiplying a number by itself. Two squared is four, three squared is nine. So, when you've fallen 3 times the time, you've fallen 9 times the distance. Very strange."

"Exactly!" Galileo said. His eyes were lit with excitement.

"Do you know why that is?" she said curiously.

He waved a hand. "I simply make observations and see patterns. I don't know what makes things fall. Newton might, though."

"Newton?" Her pulse quickened. That was the name of another of the missing books.

"Yes, but you probably already talked to him. He's in the Astronomer's Tower."

She shook her head, frowning. "I didn't see—wait, there was a locked door. Maybe he was in there?"

Galileo snapped his fingers. "You know, the last time I saw the astronomers, they left a key here." He pointed to one of the stones in the wall. "See if you can pry that stone out."

She just managed to get her fingers around the edge of the stone and pry it out. In a tiny space beyond, was a large iron key. Amazed, she pulled it out, examining it. It was iron, heavy, cold in her hands. She secured it in her bag of keys.

"Thank you!" she said.

He nodded. "Newton. I'm sure he'll have the answers you're looking for."

Science Activity:

 The Exploratorium has a musical experiment you can do to get a feel for what Galileo discovered. It's called *Falling Rhythm*. (Search 'Exploratorium Falling Rhythm to find it.) To do this activity, get a measuring tape, a cookie sheet, a long piece of rope or string, and some washers to act as weights. First, tie a weight on the string every foot. Stand on a stool and hold one end of the string, so that it dangles down, with the first weight just touching the ground. Put a cookie sheet below, to make the sound louder. Drop the string onto the cookie sheet. Listen to the pattern the falling weights make as they hit the sheet. You should notice that they hit closer and closer together, since they're speeding up. Now, untie the weights or get a new piece of string. Now tie one at the 1-inch mark, the 4-inch mark, the 9- inch mark, 16 inches (1 ft, 4 inches), 25 inches (2 ft 1 inch), 36 inches (3 ft), and 49 inches (4 ft 1 inch). Again, stand on the stool, with the string dangling. The closer-together weights should be closest to the ground. Now, drop the string and listen to the rhythm they make! It should sound like a regular drumbeat. This is because the longer things fall, the farther they go with every second.

Chapter Thirteen:
A Hopeful View

WORRY and Galileo spent the afternoon polishing lenses and tidying Galileo's workshop. He seemed very happy to have company and chattered on about math and telescopes.

"What about tides?" Worry asked. "How do those work?"

He frowned and scratched the back of his neck, dislodging his ghostly hat. "Er, well. I'm pretty sure it's because of our motion around the sun. You know how if you're carrying a bowl of soup, it sloshes around? I think that's what causes it. Maybe. It's just a guess."

Kepler put both paws over his face, but Galileo pointedly ignored him.

As evening closed in, Worry's anxiety rose. The second night of the syzygy was beginning. On the other side of the bay, Fort and her soldiers would be preparing to defend the kingdom from attacks. From more dragons. *I'm okay, Fort.* She tried to imagine Fort hearing the words. Hoped it would comfort her.

Galileo and Worry sat in the depths of the central tower, where a second great lens pointed up at the first lens. Together, the two lenses made a powerful telescope.

As they made the final adjustments, the red moon appeared, again creeping high into the sky to join the other two moons.

They sat in silence, staring up through the lenses at the magnified sky overhead. Waiting as the light in the observatory became redder.

Galileo sighed in contentment. "It's been so long since I looked through a telescope," he said softly. "For the last several years of my life, I was nearly completely blind."

Worry looked at him sympathetically.

He shrugged. "I saw more than most in my life, though. I saw farther into the solar system than any human before me. I was the first to see the moons of Jupiter." He went silent, lost again in remembering.

The red moon appeared at the edge of the lens. Worry gasped, moving closer, squinting her eyes and straining.

Bit by bit, it edged into view, until it covered the whole lens.

The details! The red surface was pockmarked with craters, and she could see every rock and ridge. "It's not smooth at all," Worry said softly.

"That surprised me, too," Galileo said. "And another of the things that disproved Aristotle. The moon and the sun weren't perfectly smooth, celestial objects like everyone thought they were."

"You don't? But your name? It was given to you by one, was it not?"

She sighed. "Yes. But she disappeared."

Galileo gasped and lifted a finger, as if he were pointing at the ceiling. "She did? I—I can't believe I didn't think of this earlier. But I believe I've heard of you."

Worry froze, her gaze lifting to his. "What do you mean you've heard of me?"

"A traveler came to visit one rainy night. She came in to get out of the storm. I—" he blushed. "I pretended to be a scary ghost for a while. Sometimes it's fun to think I'm haunting this place . . ." He scratched the side of his head. "Anyway, she was not amused. And she already knew who I was. She said she was on her way to the castle of the Scholar Knights. Where her nieces were studying."

Worry's heart stopped. She wasn't completely confident in Galileo's sense of time, but . . . did she and Hope have an aunt somewhere?

"What did she say?" Worry prodded.

"She said she'd gone to correct a mistake. You see, one of the fairy godmothers had been in an incredible rush. She'd appeared at the birth, had been about to pronounce the name, had just said the first letter, when she stopped and looked up into the sky. She'd looked suddenly terrified. She disappeared before she finished the name."

A strange sense of unreality washed over Worry. It was as if someone had slipped a giant lens in between her and the memories of her entire life. Everything looked different.

Her mouth went dry, and it took her a few tries before she was able to speak. "What was the letter?"

"W," Galileo said. "I wish I'd thought of it when you first arrived. Especially because your name is so . . . unusual."

"Depressing, you mean?" Worry said faintly, but her mind was spinning.

"Er . . . not the usual tone of the Scholar Knights. They can be a tad . . . grandiose I feel."

The fairy godmother only said the first letter. That had been her fairy godmother, Worry felt sure of it. *My name might not be Worry at all.*

"But . . . why . . . why am I . . . How did I get my name?" she wondered aloud.

"That I do not know."

What did she mean for my name to be? Worry stood, motionless, her eyes unfocused, staring straight through Galileo. *Wonder? Warmth? Warrior?* She thought back to every time she'd ever questioned herself. How often in her life had she dismissed her own thoughts as worries?

Worth? Tears sprang into her eyes.

"Thank you," she said, her throat thick with emotion. "Thank you for telling me this."

He looked at her sympathetically. "Names can be heavy burdens sometimes."

She nodded, her mind still whirling, remembering every time she'd been annoyed at herself for worrying.

"Do I . . . do I seem like . . ." she trailed off, finding herself too afraid to ask the question.

"You seem very level-headed," Galileo said, guessing at her question. "You ask interesting questions. I saw you leap into the bottomless pit of despair, you know. Not many people go in there. At least on purpose. You seem . . . thoughtful. But just because one can see possible bad outcomes doesn't mean one is overly worried, or that one should dismiss those thoughts out of hand. There might be . . . useful information in those thoughts."

Worry nodded. *What is my name? If it's not Worry, what do I think of myself as? Who am I?*

It was something she'd have to . . . consider. Maybe something would occur to her. Until then, what was most important was getting back to the castle and figuring out how to rescue Hope.

"It was lovely to meet you," she said. "Thank you again. I'm sure I'll be back soon."

His eyes lit up. "That would be wonderful! I wish you all the best in your quest, Miss W."

She smiled and, Kepler at her heels, hurried back down the steps.

Chapter Fourteen:
Newton

THE castle was buzzing with activity. Groups of heavily armed men and women jogged through the halls, lighting their way with blazing torches. Worry dodged through secret passageways and crept through halls, narrowly avoiding being noticed several times.

When she reached the main level, she emerged from a stairwell and bumped right into a guard. He looked just as shocked as she felt. He reached for her, but she stumbled back, slipping out of his grasp and scrambling away.

Her feet pounded the floor, and she dodged into the Hall of Mirrors, only a few feet in front of him. She dove behind a mirror just before he rounded the corner after her.

She could hear his heavy breathing, only a few feet away. His footsteps clicked across the stone floor towards her, pausing to peer behind each mirror he passed. He stopped right in front of the mirror behind which Worry crouched.

It was a mirror that showed your ideal hair style, and she heard a slight intake of breath, and a ruffle as he ran his fingers through his hair.

She closed her eyes, expecting at any second to feel his hand descend on her shoulder.

A tiny skittering noise reached her ears, and she opened her eyes to see the spoon she'd given the olive to.

It shot out of its labyrinth, jumping excitedly at the man's feet and pointing out the other door frantically.

"You sure?" the guard asked.

The spoon gestured frantically.

"Thanks, little guy," the guard said and ran off in the direction the spoon had pointed. Straight into the infinite loop hallway.

Worry exhaled slowly. He'd find his way out, but it would likely take hours.

"Thank you," Worry whispered. The spoon bowed its head, and she continued on her way.

At last, she made it to the Astronomy Tower.

The door was open.

Had it really only been a day and a half since she and Hope had last stood here?

Deftly, she slipped inside and approached the second, locked door.

Galileo's key fit perfectly.

She crept inside, shutting the door quietly. Kepler arrived at her side, looking uncharacteristically reverent and solemn.

He straightened his fluffy collar and looked up at her, eyes wide and excited.

They moved farther into the dark expanse. Kepler's light expanded, filling the dark corners and illuminating a large circular room.

Tapestries on every wall depicted dragons. Dragons of every shape and size and color, glittering, soaring through the skies across a background of stars and planets. Worry stared in wonder. These were not terrifying monsters. There was something joyful about the way they were depicted. Wonderous and exciting.

"Newton?" she whispered, her voice echoing through the dark, still space.

There was only silence.

Worry approached a wooden contraption in the center of the room. A wooden scaffolding surrounded a large rickety cage flanked by gears and levers. Thick chains extended into the darkness overhead.

Finally.

An elevator.

Stepping onto the central platform, Worry glanced at Kepler, who nodded. She flipped the switch.

With a groan and a great clanking of chains, the elevator lurched upwards.

Relishing the effortless upwards motion, Worry examined the walls as they went. More mathematical drawings, more paintings of dragons, some with people standing next to them. Smiling, happy people holding telescopes.

What had happened? Had the dragons and the astronomers been working together? They didn't look like evil people conspiring to commit terrible atrocities. But then, Worry didn't know anyone who had committed any atrocities, so she didn't know what they looked like.

The ride lasted a very long time. Again, as she rose higher and higher, she felt lighter and lighter. She vastly preferred this calm speed to her fall through the pit of despair. She sat cross-legged, watching the paintings go by and talking with Kepler.

"What do you think my name is?" she asked him at last.

"I don't know," he said. She was surprised not to hear a sea fact.

"Do I seem like a Warmth to you? Or maybe a Warrior?"

"Hmm . . ." he twisted his moustache. "I suppose you could be Worldly now."

"Mmm . . ." That didn't feel right. "Wit?"

"Fort would probably call you Wily."

"Or Wild," Worry added. "Am I Wacky?"

"No. You're Watchful, though."

That was too close to Worry for her liking.

The elevator gave a shudder and began to slow. Worry's heart sped up and she climbed to her feet, staring up into the darkness. A flickering light glowed up ahead. She stared at it, holding her breath and willing it to resolve into a glowing figure. Someone who would tell her how to rescue her sister.

The elevator platform lifted into an ancient workshop. Windows ringed the room, and a staircase at the far end led to a small trap door in the ceiling. Next to this, an enormous canon crouched, pointing through a hole in the ceiling. Tools lay scattered around it, like someone had been working on it recently. In between the windows were floor-to-ceiling chalkboards covered in smudged writings.

Hesitantly, Worry took a step inside, which accidentally became a short leap in the low gravity.

A roaring fire burned in a grate at one end, filling the room with flickering light and shadows. A figure stood hunched over the fire, their back turned to Worry.

"Newton?" she said hesitantly, although this was no ghost.

The figure jerked and wheeled around, her mouth dropping open.

It was Fort.

She was holding a thick, leatherbound book.

Her expression softened, a look of joy and relief crossed her face, then swiftly turned to rage.

"What—what are you doing here? I thought—"

"I'm okay. I'm sorry I tricked those people. I just had to . . . I had to know." Her eyes flicked to the book in Fort's hand. "Is that the book of Newton?"

Fort's expression hardened. "So, it really was you who stole Kepler's book. You're working with them, aren't you? How long? This whole time? I wondered why a girl without a fairy godmother was brought here. It was all lies, wasn't it?"

"What? No, of course not. I— What are you talking about?" Worry asked.

Fort moved closer to the fire; her eyes locked on Worry. "Who are you really?"

"I . . . I was going to ask you that. What is my name, really?"

"You tell me."

"I don't know!" Worry cried in frustration. "I was just talking to Galileo, who said that—"

Fort blanched, and her cheeks flushed a hectic, angry red. "So, you are conspiring with them! It's true. And you must have found a way to break the protection spell I put around Kepler, didn't you? You've been lying to me this whole time."

Worry gaped, infuriated at the unfair accusations. "Of course not! And no, but . . . but *you* were the one who put this spell on Kepler? Why?"

"To protect the world! To hold together the last vestiges of this society!" Fort's voice rose to a desperate pitch. She sounded like she might cry. "And all this time you've . . . you're the one who opened the tower. You sent your sister there on purpose, didn't you?" Fort took a step towards her.

Now Worry felt like crying. "Of course not! I'm trying to get her back! Why won't you tell me anything? I just want to know what's going on!"

Kepler was inching away from her, moving around the edge of the room, trying to get behind Fort.

Fort saw him and spun around. "You!"

Kepler took another step towards her, but Fort held up a hand and he froze, unable to take another step.

"Please, Fort," Worry said. "I swear I don't know anything. Hope wanted to break into the tower—"

"Right. Blame your sister. Convenient."

"No—I . . . I didn't mean to. I just have to get her back! I . . . Will you please tell me my real name, at least?"

"Your name is Worry," Fort said. "You came here with your sister, with only a W sewn onto your baby blanket. I paid attention, watched what you said and did, and I picked your name."

"You named me this? But . . . but what if you were wrong?"

"Clearly, I was wrong. Maybe your name was Wreckage or Woe."

Worry drew herself up taller. "Fort, that's just mean. I swear I knew nothing about the astronomers. I've been trying and trying to figure out how to get to the moon so I can get Hope back. And I'm sorry I'm messing up your plans. I completely believe that you're trying to do the right thing, but you've kept me in the dark and I have no idea what's going on!" Her fists were clenched, and she realized she was shouting.

Fort's eyes narrowed. "At the last syzygy, a horde of dragons came from the red moon. They'd been planning this with the astronomers, unbeknownst to the Scholar Knights. The astronomers wanted power. They never liked that they were always second place to the knights. They lured the scholars out of the castle, just like you lured Hope, and then they brought the dragons in for their attack." Fort was breathing heavily. "There were almost no survivors."

Worry's eyes widened. "That's horrible. Were you there?"

124

"My teachers were there. They would barely speak of it." She shook her head.

"But . . . where did the astronomers go?"

"The last of the knights were still very powerful. Those who survived, after the dragons disappeared, they attacked the astronomers, driving them into exile. They locked up the books and sealed the tower. Which you apparently figured out how to open. But even after that, no one wanted their children to join the knights anymore. They started putting wards up when their children were born, so the fairies couldn't give them names. And so, the order of the Scholar Knights began to die."

Worry struggled to make sense of all this. It felt like there were pieces missing from the story. Was it really power the astronomers had wanted? Her eyes went to the book in Fort's hand. The answers would be in there, she was sure of it. She couldn't just take Fort's word for it. Not anymore. Not after the years and years of lies.

"I want to help," Worry said. "I want to trust you." She swallowed. "Can I please just read the book?"

"These are secrets I am sworn to protect," Fort shot back. "I won't let you call the dragons back."

She lifted the book. Kepler's eyes went wide. "No, please," Worry said.

Fort tossed the book into the fire.

The ancient cover caught immediately, flames licking around its edges. Sparks of magic hissed and exploded like fireworks.

Worry felt like she was falling into the pit of despair again.

Fort turned to her. "Where's the Kepler book, Worry?"

Worry blanched and Kepler began to struggle against the invisible wall Fort had put up. His tiny paws flailed in empty space, like he was digging a hole in the air.

Instinctively, Worry clutched her bag and took a step back.

"It won't hurt him," Fort said. "The book is only a gate. It's a doorway, not a person."

She reached out a hand and stepped towards Worry.

"No," Worry said. "You can't."

But there was nowhere to run. She took another step back and found herself lifting into the air, as if she'd taken a bounding leap. The syzygy must be nearby.

Fort lunged for her as Worry drifted back down. Worry's feet hit the ground just in time for her to push off to the side, careening towards the fire. Fort sailed past, her arms swiping the empty air where Worry had been a second earlier.

She narrowly avoided crashing into the flames. She reached into the inferno and yanked the book out, immediately dropping it as the heat seared her hands.

Without thinking, she dropped, belly first, onto the ancient, flaming book, wrapping her arms around it. The flames went out. Tears pricked the corners of her eyes, seeing the charred and smoking book.

Fort approached, moving between her and the elevator.

I'm trapped.

"Kepler!" she yelled. "What do I do?"

Fort lunged for her again, sailing straight for her.

126

She can't change direction, Worry realized. Without the floor to push off from, Fort had no way to turn. Worry scooped up the book and dodged out of her way, leaping again to the far side of the room. She found herself next to the staircase below the trap door.

"Don't despair!" Kepler shrieked. His voice was strangled, as if his collar were choking him, trying to prevent him from speaking. "Whatever you do, absolutely do not despair! Like before. When you were in despair. Don't do that!"

"What?!" Worry yelled. *What is he talking about?* "Like the pit of despair?"

"Right! Definitely not that!"

"But there's not a—" she looked up at the trap door. "Oh. Oh no."

Fort's expression went livid as Worry hurled herself up the steps. She narrowly missed Worry's ankles as she yanked open the trapdoor and hurled herself out into empty space.

It was an utterly still night. The sky overhead was clear and cloudless, a vast expanse of stars and nothingness.

I wish I had time to consider this, Worry thought as she crouched and then leapt upwards with all her strength.

127

Chapter Fifteen:
The Leap and the
Truth about Gravity

IT WAS slower than falling in the pit of despair had been. Gentler. She was already slowing down, but very gradually. Drifting upward in the vast emptiness.

Slower and slower, with the world opening below her. She saw the vast, dark ocean, its surface flecked with moonlight. And Galileo's leaning tower on the island across the bay. And in the distance the hulking dark shapes of mountains.

Craning her neck, she looked up to see the red moon expanding, appearing larger and larger as she drew closer.

Minutes passed, and Worry marveled at the stars, at the castle growing smaller below.

Again, Worry was surprised at how quickly one could get bored. Gently, she opened the book of Newton, terrified that all she would see were crumbling, charred pages.

As she cracked open the cover, smoke began to pour out, billowing into the shape of a man in long robes. His hair was on fire, and he coughed, but he was scribbling something on smoky paper.

"Just a second, just a second," he said, writing furiously.

Worry waited patiently, still rising slowly into the air.

He paused to chew on the end of his quill, staring out into empty space. After a few seconds of this, he blinked, then yelped and whirled around. He looked from Worry to the ground far below, and then to the moon overhead.

"Hello," Worry said. "Are you Newton?"

He cleared his throat. "This . . . this is a dream. Or I'm dead?" He looked down at his smoking, translucent body. "Ah. Dead." He glanced back at his work in frustration. "I don't suppose you'd let me finish what I was working on?" He peered more closely at her. "You're not at all what I expected."

"You're not dead," Worry said. "The fairies made a book that lets us ask you questions."

Newton frowned. "That . . . that doesn't sound . . . like something that is scientifically possible."

"I'm not sure how it works," Worry said.

Newton looked around him again. "But . . . fairies. And . . . okay, so I'm a . . . I'm a spirit?" He poked at his ghostly stomach with a transparent finger. It went straight through. "Oh. Oh no. I am going to have to rethink so many things now . . ." He looked both overwhelmed and fascinated. "But fourth rule of reasoning! New phenomena mean we rethink the ideas!"

"If it helps, my world is different than your world."

Newton scratched his chin. "Well, third rule of reasoning: if something is a physical law in one place it's a physical law everywhere. So . . . but, what do you mean a different world? Oh, the New World? Virginia? New Spain?"

"Ummm . . . maybe? To be honest I don't know."

"Huh." Newton put his hands on his hips and surveyed the empty void around them. "Well, this truly is most fascinating." He looked down at the planet they were slowly drifting away from, and then up at the moon they were approaching. "Are we . . . in the heavens?"

"I think so, yes."

"And you're sure I'm not dead?"

"I'm not sure of anything at the moment."

"Fair enough. Been there myself plenty of times. What did you say your name was?"

Worry opened her mouth, but something made her pause. She didn't want to give the name that Fort had given her. It was a name that had made her doubt her own thoughts her whole life. She couldn't guess what the fairy had wanted to name her, but part of her didn't want that name anyway. It was another name to try to live up to, or to fight against. A name with pressure and assumptions and roles. "I'm Abigail," she said, feeling a warm glow in her stomach that might have just been nausea caused by currently being a human projectile.

"Lovely to meet you, Abigail," Newton said. He looked again at the moon. "Fascinating. Absolutely fascinating. What is happening?"

"I jumped, and now I seem to be floating towards the moon. I'm hoping to make it there, but I don't know if I will. Do you know?"

"Oh, certainly. I do not know but I can easily calculate it. What speed did you jump with? What are the masses of

130

your planet and moons? What is the distance between their centers?"

"Umm..."

Newton frowned. "We can't answer any questions without data! An understanding of the world requires an understanding of numbers."

Abigail nodded. "Galileo said something like that, too."

Newton's face lit up. "Galileo?!"

"Oh, yes, I just spoke with him. Do you know him?"

Newton sat down cross-legged, propped his elbows on his knees and his chin in his hands. His hair still burned merrily. "I wish. I love Galileo. He died the year before I was born, unfortunately. So close! But I've read all his works." He sighed dreamily. "He was so smart. Lots of evidence for the ideas of Copernicus, which I love. The sun being the center of the universe and the Earth travelling around it. In elliptical orbits, as Kepler discovered."

"Oh, you know Kepler, too?"

"No, he also passed before I was born. How do you know him?"

"He's my cat."

Newton considered this.

"I... I think I will have to treat this as a very strange dream. I'm not sure I'm quite ready to throw out my whole Principia Mathematica. Despite the Fourth Rule of Reasoning."

"That's understandable," Abigail said. She glanced up at the moon again. "Can you tell me what's happening? I really need to make it to that moon. My sister's there. She was kidnapped. Aristotle said that maybe she just belongs there."

Newton rolled his eyes. "My apologies for the eye roll. That was very impolite of me. Aristotle was extremely brilliant. It's amazing, really. Did you study Aristotle in school? I did. His ideas were still incredibly popular in my time, the late 1600's, even though he was writing in the 4th century BCE. Isn't that wild? Two thousand years later! But he used too much philosophy in his attempts to understand the natural world, in my opinion. True understanding requires experimentation. That's where it's at."

"I wasn't allowed to go to school."

"Oh, because you're a girl?"

"What? No. Why would that matter? Because I don't have a fairy godmother."

"Huh. An equally illogical reason, I suppose." He paused. "Is my hair on fire?"

His hair sent off a cheerful shower of sparks.

"Yes, it is. So . . . if the moon isn't celestial and, in the heavens, because it's made of aether and destined to be there . . . why is it there?"

Newton grinned. "Well! Let me tell you! It's pretty incredible, really. I was surprised when I figured it out."

Abigail lifted her eyebrows.

Newton continued. "One of my greatest accomplishments, and I have many, many accomplishments, was my Law of Universal Gravitation."

"What's that?" Also, why did everyone have laws? She supposed it was the need for certainty. As someone currently floating farther and farther away from everything she'd ever known, out into an infinite void, towards a strange new world inhabited by dragons, she could understand the desire for certainty.

"Well, it turns out that everything is attracted to everything else."

"What? What do you mean?"

Newton rummaged in his pockets and pulled out two more quills. He held them up at arm's length. "If I let go of these two quills, they would ever so slowly start to move towards one another."

"But . . . I've never seen anything like that."

"Well, no, you wouldn't have. And excellent question! Well done! Using your observations to discern the truth! Lovely. But be careful, because things are complicated. Sometimes things are so gradual that we can't perceive them, or there are other phenomena getting in the way."

"Like air resistance?"

Newton looked even more impressed. "Yes, exactly like that."

"That's why Aristotle thought bigger things fell faster."

Newton pointed at her. "Well done! Wow! Yes!"

Abigail felt like she must be glowing as much as Kepler did when he was near his book.

"Anyway, this attraction that all mass has for all other mass, it's very weak. So tiny that we can't notice it in our everyday life. But it's there." He pointed down at the planet. "See how enormous it is? That's why we can feel the effects of gravity. The more mass there is, the greater the force." He cleared his throat. "Apologies. Force is simply a push or a pull. People really were upset at my idea of gravity, though. Because usually a force is an obvious push or a pull. You have to be touching something. But gravity doesn't work that way. It's called "action at a distance" and it's a fairly strange idea."

"I can see why. How do things pull on each other without touching?"

"I have no idea! But that's fine. These things are complicated. It took two thousand years, and many brilliant scientists—Kepler, Galileo, Copernicus," he cleared his throat again, "me . . . to refine and change his ideas based on our experiments. I'm sure people will figure it out in the future."

"Wow . . . so all of this . . . every time anything falls . . . it's because mass is attracted to mass . . ."

"Yes, which is why things all go the same speed, if you ignore air resistance. The more massive something is, the harder it is to get it to speed up—that's my second law, you know—but also, the more massive something is the more gravitational force it experiences. Those two things balance out exactly and they speed up—accelerate—in exactly the same way."

"Amazing! But . . . why don't the moons crash into our planet?"

"Moons? You have several? Fascinating. We only have one. But that's something pretty incredible. The answer is that the moon is always falling."

"But . . . if it's always falling, then why doesn't it . . ."

"Why doesn't it hit your planet? Well, because it's falling *around* your planet. Imagine standing on the surface of your planet. You throw a ball as far as you can. Maybe from the top of that giant tower you have."

"Okay, I can imagine that."

"Your planet is curved, like all planets. So, as the ball travels in a straight line, the ground is curving down away from it. If you threw it fast enough, then the speed at which it fell would be exactly equal to the speed at which the ground was curving away from it."

"That's . . . that's so strange!"

"Indeed. So, your moons are all constantly falling towards you, but because they're going around your planet, the ground is always falling away. Like a dog trying to chase its tail."

"But . . . one of our moons moves and the other two are in the same place all the time."

"Ah, no, they only look that way. You have daytime and nighttime on your world, do you not?"

"Yes."

"Well, that's because your planet is spinning."

"Ohhh . . . So, our planet is spinning, but the moons are going around at exactly the right speed that they look like they're staying in the same place. That's so strange."

"Yes, the world is a strange, amazing, magical place. Even without fairy godmothers!"

"But why did I feel so light when I was at the top of the tower during the syzygy?"

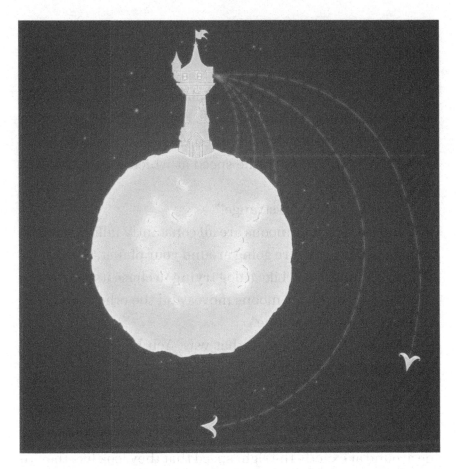

"I'm going to make some assumptions here, but that was likely because the gravity of the moons was pulling you upwards.
That's what's happening now. The gravity of your planet is
pulling you down, and the gravity of your moons—which is
weaker because they are smaller and farther away—is pulling
you up."

"So, am I going to make it? I mean, I know you don't have
numbers, but . . . any guesses?"

136

"Well, it all depends on what the speed of your jump was. One thing working in your favor is that gravity gets weaker as you get farther away. It's what we call an Inverse Square Law. If you get twice as far away, gravity gets one fourth as strong."

"Oh, kind of the like the squaring thing with the distance something falls?"

"Yes, that's a square law as well, but the distance is increasing rather than decreasing, in that case. Here, gravity decreases as we get farther away. It all depends on whether you jumped fast enough. If you did, then at some point we'll reach a place where the force of gravity from your moons is greater than the force of gravity from your planet. If you can get to that tipping point, you'll start to fall towards the moon."

Abigail blanched. "How fast will I fall?"

"Well, generally when we throw things upwards, they end up back where they started, going exactly the same speed. But in your case, you jumped from a tower, which means you've got farther to fall on the other side. But also, the moons are smaller, so their gravity is weaker." He shrugged and lifted his hands, palms upwards. "It's complicated! I really can't say how fast you'll be going."

His smoky form shifted, as if an invisible breeze were blowing him away. He dissolved into eddies and then reformed.

"Whew, this book of yours doesn't seem to work all that well."

"Fort burned it."

"Ah. Well, that explains my hair." He scratched his head and stared up at the slowly approaching moon. "I wonder what having three moons does to your tides . . ."

Abigail perked up. "So, the moons do cause the tides?"

"Oh yes indeed. As I said, gravity pulls on all matter. Oceans are matter, and they move much more easily than rock and soil do. In my world, we have a single moon. The pull of the moon and the sun combine to make the tides. Yours must be complicated! Although, the fact that two of your moons are geosynchronous—they stay in the same spot in the sky—might make it simpler. Hard to say!"

Abigail was beginning to get a sense of just how complicated the world could be. Just how much tiny variables could change our perceptions and make understanding anything so difficult. It was much easier to jump to conclusions about things. To assume things were as simple as they looked. That tides were blown by winds and the planet was the center of the universe because everything looked like it spun around them. It had taken two thousand years of very smart people taking very careful measurements to figure out that that wasn't the case. And even the great Galileo was wrong about tides.

I wonder what I'm wrong about, Abigail thought. And this time she didn't dismiss the thought as pointless worrying, but something worth considering.

"But you know," Newton said casually, "I'm not sure it's gravity you need to worry about in this situation."

"No? Why's that?"

"Well—and I don't know how things work in your world—but in mine, air gets thinner as you get higher. At some point you should reach a place with very little or no air."

"That sounds bad." She took an experimental breath. The air did feel thinner. Was she lightheaded? She thought she might be, she just hadn't noticed.

"Quite, yes. But . . . well, perhaps you will discover otherwise!"

He cleared his throat. "The other—small—problem is that the moon is moving quite rapidly. As I said, it is orbiting. Moving horizontally at a very high speed to keep from falling into your planet . . . That might pose a problem for you as well . . ."

"Ummm . . ."

"Imagine jumping onto a galloping horse. If that horse were galloping at two thousand miles per hour."

"That doesn't seem like it would work well."

"No, not at all. But you weren't entirely stopped. You were spinning along with the surface of your planet . . . anyway, like I said, I really wish I knew the masses and distances involved here . . . I feel like I'm alarming you."

"Oh, no. I'm fine," Abigail said, breathing a bit more rapidly than was necessary, trying to tell whether the air was disappearing. "Just . . . wishing I'd taken a few more measurements before jumping . . ."

Newton nodded. "Yes . . . on the other hand, sometimes we do have to just try things."

Abigail looked down at her fingers. Were the tips blue?

"Any ideas?" she asked Newton. "What should I do now?"

The fire on the side of his head gave a little pop and a shower of sparks rained down.

"Hmm . . ." he said. "Well, maybe if you . . ."

The smoke shuddered, and his form dissolved like a whisp of cloud on a windy day.

"Newton?" Abigail closed the book and opened it again. "Newton, are you there?"

Nothing.

A wave of dizziness washed over her, and she took a few panicked breaths. The air felt thinner, colder, she struggled to breathe.

I really should have thought this through. She panicked, struggling with all her might to draw the thin air into her lungs. *Hope made it. I can make it.*

The red moon swirled in front of her, like an apparition taunting her.

Hope, she thought muzzily. Her eyelids began to close.

Two faint pops jolted her awake. Something warm and sparkling surrounded her, and suddenly there was air again. Thick and breathable and lifegiving.

The spots and flashes faded from her vision and, shaking her head, she looked around to see Rose, pink and gold and sparkling with gossamer dragonfly wings, and Fern, green and clothed in tendrils of delicate moss and surrounded by glittering dewdrops and rainbows.

They didn't look at her, but they waved their wands, gently tending to the sphere that surrounded her.

Aristotle would have liked this, she thought dizzily.

The moon was getting larger, but she was moving so slowly she was nearly stopped.

I'm not going to make it. I'm going to stop and fall back.

But, like a ball rolling over a hill, she seemed to reach some invisible peak over which she gently toppled.

Then, just as gradually, she was picking up speed again.

Suddenly, up was down and down was up.

She'd been flying upwards, up from the surface of her planet, into the sky, but now, everything had reversed. Down was the direction of the red moon, and she was falling towards it, gaining speed.

How strange, she thought. *I thought down was . . . down. But it's actually . . . towards the . . . the biggest thing nearby?* She wasn't sure.

But she was picking up speed.

At first it wasn't too much. When she'd gone about as far down as she'd originally gone up, she was going slower than when she'd first jumped. But after that she gradually picked up speed. The ocean she'd seen from Galileo's telescope sped towards her.

Sarah Allen

Gravity Simulation:

Play around with gravity! Follow the link below or search for "Phet Gravitational Force" to try out a little simulation of what gravity is like. You'll see two spheres, like planets. There are black arrows at the top, pointing towards each other. These arrows show you how strong the gravitational force is between the objects. You can also tell because the stick figure people are holding the masses apart. If gravity gets stronger, they'll have to pull harder.

Try dragging one of the masses back and forth. Does that affect the strength of gravity?

Now play around with the mass sliders. If you make one bigger or smaller, does that change both the arrows or only one?

Is there a way to make the two arrows have different amounts of force or are they always the same? Try making it as hard as possible for the two stick people. What do you need to change about the mass and the distance to make the force of gravity as big as possible? What about as easy as possible? https://phet.colorado.edu/sims/html/gravity-force-lab/latest/gravity-force-lab_all.html

Chapter Sixteen:
Finding Hope

THE fairy bubble protected her.

She splashed into the water, the force of her impact taking her several feet underwater. A luminous jellyfish stared at her wiggling its tentacles, and then the bubble shot back up, popping above the waves and settling down to float.

A swift current pulled it along until it bumped up against some shallow rocks and popped.

Abigail splashed down into the water, quickly getting her feet under her and standing.

The water was about knee deep, extending as far as she could see in all directions.

It was also daylight.

A pleasant, salty breeze was blowing, and silver and orange fish leapt from the waves, snapping bugs out of the air.

Looking back up the way she had come, Abigail saw an incredible sight. Her own planet, bright and silver and green with life, mostly in shadow, but glowing at the edges.

Behind it was the sun, glowing brightly, but looking like a crescent moon, partially eclipsed by her own planet. Her jaw dropped and she quickly looked away, the brightness hurting her eyes.

This was what the syzygy looked like from the red moon. Not the ominous nighttime alignment of colorful spheres, but a shadowy silver planet eclipsing the sun.

Where was Hope?

Shading her eyes with her hand, she scanned the horizon.

She didn't have time to search the whole moon. At least the water was smooth and shallow, and she could see for miles in every direction. Picking a direction at random, she splashed through the clear water, sending ripples out in every direction.

The gravity was so light here that every step sent her sailing through the air. It was almost like flying. She leapt, gliding several feet before slowly splashing down. It almost felt like she could keep floating forever.

Newton had said that if you threw something fast enough, it would orbit. Even jumping as hard as she could, she still splashed back down. Curious, though, she pulled a coin from her bag and threw it as hard as she could. To her astonishment, it sailed over the horizon. She stood, hands on hips, watching the place where it had disappeared, until, moments later, something whacked into her back.

She groaned, spinning around, panicked and expecting to see the dragon. But there was no one behind her.

Glinting in the water below her was the coin. It hadn't travelled all the way around the moon, had it?

144

She threw it again in another direction, with exactly the same speed.

This time, she spun around, scanning the smooth horizon.

Not long after, it came gliding up around towards her. She caught it deftly, her eyebrows lifting. Then she grinned.

Making a very slight turn, she threw the coin again. Again, she caught it when it came around the other side.

"This moon really is smooth," she muttered to herself.

She repeated the process for a few minutes, throwing it all the way around the moon again and again until one time, it didn't return.

Maybe I didn't throw it fast enough, she thought. Her arm was getting tired. She tried again with another coin. It still didn't return. That meant it had hit something. Like an island.

Hoping she was going the right way, Abigail sprinted off in the direction she'd thrown the coin that hadn't returned. She took great leaping strides, soaring over the surface of the water.

A thin column of dark smoke appeared in the distance. She splashed towards it, a rising current now dragging at her knees, and an island materialized. She stared at it, open-mouthed. It was the island she'd seen through Galileo's telescope. She'd made it.

The water now rose to her mid thighs, and she struggled along, slipping in the sand and waving her arms as she went. The red island grew, getting taller as she approached.

She arrived at the base of a sheer red cliff, extending straight upwards. Turning right, she began to make her way around the island, looking for a way inside.

Seabirds nested in the cliffs, diving and calling to one another.

Something gold glinted, catching Abigail's attention.

There, at the foot of the great red cliff, half-submerged in the water, was a solid gold cage with thick bars. Sitting on a large stone in the center of the cage, her knees drawn up to her chest, her clothes and hair soaked, was Hope.

"Hope!" Abigail called, overjoyed, splashing towards her sister.

"Worry?" Hope shivered and stood, leaning against the bars. "What are you doing here? How did you get here?"

Abigail reached through the bars, wrapping her arms around her sister and holding her tight. "I jumped. Are you okay?"

"You . . . you jumped?" Hope leaned back, her blue eyes wide, taking in her sister. "I'm okay, but . . . I tried to escape. The dragon was keeping me up on the top of the island, but at the last syzygy, I ran. It caught me and locked me in here."

Abigail leaned back, too, scanning the area for any sign of the dragon. She noticed horizontal lines on the sheer red cliff, and her stomach went cold. Those were water lines. Showing how high the tide usually rose. And they were even with the top of the cage. Would the tide be higher or lower than usual during a syzygy?

"Hope, how long have you been in here? How high does the water get?"

Her sister swallowed hard. "Umm . . . only a few hours. The water was lower before." Her voice quavered. "All this was bare rock a while ago. I guess I hadn't . . . hadn't noticed."

Abigail pulled back and frantically began searching for a way to open the cage.

"The door's over there," Hope said, pointing. "But she melted it shut. There's no key."

Hope wrapped her arms around her soaked and tattered pink dress.

"Don't worry," Abigail said. "I'll get you out."

Again, her sister gave her that look: surprised, like she was meeting a stranger.

Abigail ran her hands quickly over every bar, testing and tugging on it, but the cage was solid. She didn't have anything to pry it open with, either. She tried shaking the cage, thinking she could move the whole thing, but it wouldn't budge.

Clenching her fists, which were cold and clammy from the saltwater, she looked up at the cliff. "Where's the dragon?"

Hope's eyebrows climbed higher into her disheveled silver hair. "You'd better get out of here. It'll only lock you up, too, Worry."

Abigail pulled her sister into another quicky hug, the gold bars cold and hard between them.

"Hold on for just a little longer, okay?" she said. "I promise I'm going to figure out a way to get you out of there."

Science Note

How high will the tide go? You might have noticed in the tide charts that they change from day to day and month to month. What affects how deep the tides will be? Will the tide be higher or lower than usual during the syzygy?

It turns out that the gravity from the sun and the moon together create our tides. Interestingly, the moon creates two high tides, one where it is, and one on the other side of the Earth. This is because gravity gets weaker as you get farther away. The moon pulls on the water nearest to it, lifting it up, but it also pulls on the Earth, pulling it slightly towards it. It pulls less on the water on the far side, which gets left behind, creating another high tide. The sun does the same thing, although it has less of an effect because it's farther away. Check out the Exploratorium video *Dance of the Tides* to see a visual of how this works.

On Earth, we have a similar situation to the syzygy, which is when the sun, moon, and earth are in alignment. We call this a 'spring tide'. There is also what's called a "neap tide" which is when the moon is not in alignment with the sun but is instead at a right angle. There's a cool simulation of how this works here: https://beltoforion.de/en/tides/simulation.php. In the simulation, try clicking "neap tide" and "spring tide" one at a time. What do you notice about the tidal bulge? (The blue oval shape represents the ocean. The more stretched it gets, the higher the tide will be.)

During the syzygy on Abigail's planet, the tide will probably be similar to the spring tide, because all the planets and the sun are in alignment, meaning they all work together to make the tide bigger.

But many more factors influence the tides. Some places on Earth only have one high tide, because of the way the Earth's axis of rotation is tilted. The shape of the coastline affects the tides, too, as does the rotation of the Earth and the positions of the sun and moon. Because of this, high tides can be before or after the moon is at its highest point and can vary a lot from day to day and month to month! Complicated! No wonder it took so long for us to figure it out.

You can also watch Neil deGrasse Tyson talk about the tides on YouTube: *"Neil deGrasse Tyson Explains the Tides."*

Chapter Seventeen:
The Dragon's Lair

FOLLOWING Hope's directions, Abigail jogged around the base of the island until she came to a gaping maw of a cave. The opening extended forty feet overhead. The tide made a roaring, sucking noise as it swept in and out of the cave. Stalactites stabbed down like fangs.

Abigail took a deep breath, straining her ears for any sound, and made her way inside.

It was an echoing, hollow place. A warren of tunnels leading up through the center of the island. A cool wind brushed ghostly whispers into her mind.

The crash of the ocean receded as she moved deeper into the lair. The walls were crystal, like dark corroded mirrors encrusted with salt. Here and there one gave a flicker or burst of light. One cracked in half right as she passed, and she flinched. For a moment, she stood there, shaking, her breath coming in short gasps. But she thought of her sister, trapped outside. She took a deep breath and stood up straighter.

I don't know what's in here, but whatever it is, I will figure it out.

The cave smelled like burned seaweed and the dripping of water sounded like footsteps.

She passed ancient empty halls and a place where enormous talons had scraped deep gouges into the walls. She avoided looking at them too closely.

On tiptoe, Abigail climbed higher, following the largest branch of the tunnel as it wound up and down and around.

A great groan echoed through the space, and Abigail clapped her hands over her ears as two more lifeless crystals shattered.

Pressing close to the wall and crouching, she crept forwards.

The tunnel opened out into a massive cavern. Columns thicker than tree trunks stretched a hundred feet into the air, supporting an arched ceiling. Into this ceiling were stone carvings of dragons in flight. Their eyes and talons and tails encrusted with jewels.

It was like a massive library with stories and stories of shelves, all with arched balconies and nooks and statues of fairies. But there was not a single book. The whole place was empty. Nothing rested on the shelves. No jewels, no books, no treasures of any kind.

A great hole in the ceiling was open to the sky above, and a column of sunlight angled nearly straight down, expanding like a spotlight and illuminating a small section of floor below.

In this tiny column of sunlight lay the dragon.

Its long, scaled tail with six silver spikes was curled around its body. Its eyes were closed, and its muscular arms were wrapped tightly around something Abigail couldn't quite make out.

Strangely, it reminded her of Fort, clutching her blankets to her chest as she slept.

The dragon gave another earsplitting groan, and a thick tear leaked out of the corner of one scaly eye.

The dragon was crying.

Ever so quietly, barely breathing, Abigail descended a set of steps.

Her boot dislodged a pebble, which rolled and then tumbled down, the noise of its fall echoing painfully loudly. Abigail froze.

The scaly eyelid shot open, the amethyst eye with its red pupil fixed directly on her.

The legs uncoiled, the talons flexed, the leathery wings lifted, their spikes extending. Terror shot through her as the creature sent a burst of fire over her head, narrowly missing her.

Abigail raised her hands high, fixing the dragon with a pleading stare. "Um, hello? I'm sorry to bother you. Please, could I speak with you?"

The dragon's talons scored deep grooves in the stone, and it opened its jaws. Flames licked out of its mouth, curling through its spikes of charred teeth.

Fear locked Abigail in place.

Between its feet were two oblong chunks of stone, each giving off a faint glow. One pink, one blue.

The bright purple eye followed her gaze to the stones. The pupil contracted to a tiny slit, and the dragon dug its talons further into the stone, giving an earsplitting roar. Dust and chunks of stone rained down from the ceiling.

Abigail threw her arms over her head but stood her ground.

"I'm sorry to barge in like this," she yelled at the top of her voice. "Could I please speak with you for a moment?"

Another burst of fire shot overhead, and the dragon stalked towards her, opening its massive jaws.

Abigail winced and dodged behind one of the enormous columns. She peeked around the column and saw the dragon stamping on the floor, moving a few feet towards her, and then back to the rocks again. As if unwilling to leave them. As if it were protecting them. Like a bird might protect its eggs.

The dragon's eyes were wide, and it scanned the upper reaches of the cavern, looking from the opening in the ceiling to the various tunnel entrances. It shot another quick blast of fire at Abigail, but then did a quick spin, whirling around and looking this way and that, ready for an attack from all sides.

"I'm the only one here!" Abigail shouted, then wondered whether that had been the best thing to reveal. Luckily the dragon clearly didn't believe her.

Were its forelegs trembling? She'd seen a dog's legs shake like that once, after it had been attacked by a large eagle.

"Sorry to frighten you!" Abigail tried.

This seemed to have an effect, but not the one she'd hoped for. The dragon faced her and charged. The ground quaked with every pounding step, its muscular tail slashed behind it, and flames exploded from its mouth.

It closed the distance between them with blinding speed. Abigail didn't even have time to flinch. Her mouth was open, her eyes wide as the monster sped towards her.

At the last second, a tiny, sparkling blue light zipped in between them.

"Endure, wait!"

Abigail's stomach and arms felt like they were suddenly filled with champagne. Bubbly and sparkling.

The dragon skidded to a stop, only feet from the column Abigail crouched behind.

In between them was a tiny blue fairy.

She had shoes made of hermit crab shells, curling at the points, a tiny crown of starfish, and a dusting of blue sparkles on her skin. Earrings made of polished sea glass adorned her tiny, pointed ears, and her gossamer wings were edged with sea foam.

"It's happening again, Bluebell," the dragon said, its voice a low growl. "They've come to destroy the last of the eggs."

"No, it's okay. I promise. This is her; this is Wisdom."

Bluebell turned and smiled, her blue eyes locking with Abigail's. Abigail felt like there had been a piece of herself missing all these years, she just hadn't realized what it was. This was her fairy godmother. She was sure of it.

Slowly, she registered what the fairy had called her.

"Wisdom?" she asked. "You named me Wisdom?"

The dragon shifted its massive bulk and darted a terrified glance back at its eggs.

Bluebell frowned, giving her a polite smile. "Yes, of course. You . . . you didn't know your name? I announced it." She pulled her wand anxiously to her chest, gripping it with both hands.

Abigail explained what she'd thought her name was, and why. Bluebell's polite smile faltered. "Oh my. Oh . . . oh I am so sorry. I . . . I was in a rush to . . . well, to get here . . ." Her pointed ears drooped.

"Whoa," Abigail said, her head spinning, imagining what her life might have been like if she'd thought of herself as Wisdom. At first, it felt powerful, but then, an equal amount of pressure set in. Like every thought she had must be perfect, well-considered. Like she needed to learn as much as possible about everything and then analyze all that information until she found the absolute best solution. It was paralyzing.

I'd rather just be Abigail, she thought.

Did Hope feel this way? It must be a lot of pressure to feel like you needed to be optimistic all the time. Especially optimistic for the sake of others.

Hope. Her stomach dropped.

"Bluebell, Hope's trapped in a cage outside." But the fairy must know that already.

Bluebell's hands twisted more tightly on her wand. "Yes, I know," she said grimly. She turned to the dragon. "Endure, please, I've told you. Hope and Wisdom are here to help. To end all this. To make things safe for your eggs."

She glanced pleadingly at Abigail.

Abigail locked eyes with the dragon, who was watching her distrustfully. "Your name is Endure?"

The dragon blinked; two sets of eyelids flicking across its corneas. She shuffled back a few steps, closer to the eggs. "It is."

"Why are you called Endure?"

She lowered her head a fraction of an inch. "I was a hatchling when the knights turned on us. I did not have a name yet." Her gaze made another piercing survey of the room, looking for threats.

"What do you mean, when the knights turned on you?" Abigail asked.

"First, only a single egg was missing. Stolen. A terrible betrayal. But then the rest came. They attacked us here, destroying all our eggs except these two, which I managed to hide. Many dragons were lost, then." She hung her head, and her voice quaked. "Only a few, very old dragons remained. They named me, a tiny hatchling, Endure. It would be up to me to continue the line of the dragons, to watch over the eggs. To endure. They warned me that, when the planet covered the sun again and our world went dark, the knights would be back to destroy the last of us. Slowly, one by one, the old dragons died, and only I was left."

"That sounds so lonely," Abigail said. "And terrible. I'm so sorry."

Endure lifted her chin, her face tightening. "It is simply how things are. And I have watched over the eggs all these years, waiting until they are ready to hatch. But then the sky darkened, and the great sphere in the sky covered the sun. The ancient pathway between the worlds opened, making flight between very easy. I couldn't just cower in fear. I went to go see. And there I saw you and your sister. I thought you must be preparing an attack." She ran a large talon along a crack in the floor. "I wasn't thinking. I . . . I thought that maybe if I had one of yours, I could bargain . . . But then I didn't know what to do with her. I learned you'd all but forgotten about us. Then I realized that others might come looking for her, or she might go back and divulge what she'd found." She closed her eyes, grimacing. "I might have invited exactly what I'd feared."

"The knights attacked you first?" Abigail couldn't quite believe that. There had to be more going on. Why was everything so complicated?

"Yes." Endure's voice was firm.

Abigail took a few—very slow—steps towards Endure. She gently extended a hand and laid it on the dragon's shoulder.

Endure's eyes shot open, and she leaped backwards. After a few panicked breaths, she relaxed.

"Wow. That is . . . that is so awful. I'm so sorry we scared you by going up into the tower."

Endure eyed her warily.

Abigail turned to Bluebell. "But why are you here?"

"Dragon eggs can't survive without fairies," she said simply. "We have an ancient pact with the dragons. We care for their eggs, and in turn they assist our knights."

"Is that why Fern lied to Fort about me being under the bed?" Abigail asked.

"You were under my bed?"

Fort's voice rang out through the empty cavern as she stepped out of the shadows, swinging her sword. Fern fluttered anxiously at her shoulder, trailing green sparks.

"Fort! How did you—"

"I jumped, just like you did."

Endure froze in a crouch, her eyes wide and terrified as she watched Fort approach. It was strange to see something so huge and powerful look so scared.

"When were you under my bed?"

Abigail swallowed hard. "Yesterday. Right after I stole Kepler's book."

Fort's face was hard as stone.

"I'm sorry," Fern said in a high, pinched voice. "I promise I've never done anything like that before."

"Except that you knew there was another fairy up here, protecting the dragon that attacked the knights, that destroyed our order?"

Abigail felt desperately sorry for Fort. Now that Abigail knew what it felt like to have a fairy godmother, she couldn't imagine what it would feel like to learn that her fairy had been lying to her. And she definitely knew what it felt like to not understand what was happening.

"Fort, I think there's more going on here than you and I know," Abigail said loudly.

Fort was about to speak, but she took a step closer to the eggs, and Endure suddenly lunged for her, fire blossoming from her jaws.

"Endure, no!" the fairies shrieked.

She swung her great, spiked tail at Fort, but Fort lifted her hands, and a ball of bright green energy surrounded the dragon.

Endure slowed, as if she were encased in glowing green honey. She thrashed and struggled, and Fort grimaced, sweat pouring down her cheeks. Her jaw clenched and she took another labored step towards the eggs.

Abigail's mind spun. *I have to stop this. I don't know what's right, I don't know who started this, I don't know if the dragons really are a threat to the knights or if it's the other way around, or what the astronomers had to do with all this.* No one was listening to her, and in one more second Fort would reach the eggs.

Someone had to stop this, but the fairies weren't doing anything, and both Fort and Endure were too terrified to listen to one another let alone Abigail. She had to make them stop, had to make them pause and listen and try to figure out what had really happened. She swallowed hard and glanced at Bluebell. Her fairy godmother. *I have a fairy godmother,* she thought. *I'm a Scholar Knight now. And I am going to stop this.*

Fort took another shaking step towards the eggs. Endure thrashed against the green glowing sphere, which flickered in and out.

Abigail sprinted between them, scooped up the eggs, and jumped.

With gravity so weak, she shot upwards, straight for the opening in the ceiling.

Fort yelled, Endure roared, but Abigail didn't look down.

She was losing speed as she went, but only gradually, and she shot through the hole in the ceiling easily, then drifted back down to land next to the opening.

She stood on the top of the island, a space of bare, red rock about fifty feet across.

Clutching the eggs, she ran to the edge. She needed more time. An idea hit her, and she grabbed a couple of small rocks, throwing them horizontally off the cliff.

Seconds later, both Fort and Endure—no longer trapped—flew through the opening. Fort stumbled, but got her feet under her quickly and, raising her sword, sprinted towards Abigail.

Endure lunged for them in a blast of fire. Fort sent a blast of glowing green energy at her again, but this time it only encased the dragon's wings. She couldn't fly, but she could still attack.

"Wait!!" Abigail shouted, holding the eggs over the edge, threatening to drop them. Endure skidded to a stop, her face a mask of rage.

The fairies fluttered about anxiously.

"Wisdom, please, don't do that," Bluebell said. "The dragons didn't start this conflict. I really don't think they did."

Sarah Allen

"The knights absolutely didn't start this, either!" Fort shouted. "If we let the dragons continue, they'll destroy what's left of us. They can't be trusted. They'll betray us again, Worry."

Abigail cleared her throat. "My name," she said, "is Abigail. And we are going to talk about this and figure things out."

Fort lifted her sword and advanced. "No. They could hatch any minute. I can barely hold off one dragon. I can't fight three. You, me, Hope. We'll all be gone."

On the far side of the island, Abigail saw what she'd been hoping to see. Three rocks appearing on the horizon. Thanks to Newton, she knew why.

"Okay, just hang on one second," she insisted.

"No," Fort said, raising her sword high, preparing to swing for the eggs.

Abigail threw the eggs horizontally off the top of the island, at exactly the same speed she'd thrown the rocks. Thanks to Galileo, she knew it wouldn't matter that their masses were different.

The dragon gave a panicked roar, but it couldn't fly.

"Don't worry!" Abigail shouted, "They'll be back! They're perfectly fine. They're orbiting. We just need a little more time to figure this out."

Endure glanced from her to the eggs, looking deeply skeptical, but the eggs did seem to be peacefully floating along in the low gravity.

Fort's sword clanged against the ground, and she gave a groan of frustration.

"I never, ever, ever should have taken you in."

Abigail gave a quick glance over the side. She could just make out Hope's cage from here. The water was several feet deeper, nearly up to Hope's neck.

Better hurry.

From her bag, she whipped out Kepler's book.

"Bluebell, I need your help," she said, and the fairy was at her side instantly. "A Scholar Knight made this enchantment. Help me break it."

"No!" Fort said, but Kepler jumped through her stomach, up in front of her eyes. Fort yelped and tried to bat him away. But her hands passed straight through him.

Abigail instinctively placed her palm flat on the book. With Bluebell at her side, she could suddenly sense the enchantment that wove around and through it. That sparkling, joyful feeling again filled her arms and stomach, and Abigail wanted to laugh. This was what magic felt like?

Guided by Bluebell, Abigail felt her own source of magic. It did have a sense of wisdom about it, but there was also something Abigail-like there, too, she was sure. It poured up like water dancing off a waterfall, sending up sprays and rainbows. The enchantment dissolved.

Grinning, feeling like she'd just tasted the best cookie ever, Abigail looked at Kepler. He'd dropped to the ground and was standing, feet splayed, a look of surprise and delight on his face.

"Kepler?" she asked. "Are you free?"

He straightened his back, adjusted his moustache, and fixed her with a serious look.

"Electric eels can produce a shock of six hundred volts," he commented.

Abigail's face fell.

He grinned slyly. "Just kidding. Couldn't resist, sorry. Tides are caused by the moon! Planets travel in elliptical orbits! The time it takes them to go around the sun depends on how far away they are!" He hopped into the air, doing a flip. "Ah I can't tell you how good it feels to say that! When Aristotle was talking about crystal spheres, I thought I was going to catch on fire."

Abigail laughed.

"Don't listen to him!" Fort said. "He's working with the astronomers!"

"Astronomers can never be trusted!" Endure growled.

They glanced at one another, surprised to be in agreement.

"Kepler?" Abigail asked.

He adjusted his fluffy collar and turned to Fort and the dragon. "It was the astronomers."

Fort kept her sword raised.

"For a long while, the castle was home to both the Scholar Knights and the League of Astronomers. There was a rivalry between the astronomers and the knights, though. The astronomers were jealous of the knights. Not only could the knights work magic, but every scholar had not only a fairy godmother, but a dragon as well."

Fort's jaw dropped and her sword tip lowered. She darted a glance at Endure who frowned suspiciously. Again, they looked surprisingly similar, Abigail thought.

Kepler went on. "The knights and the dragons worked together for centuries. Er, you might have noticed your names are slightly similar. In order to endure, one must have fortitude, you might say. You do have certain commonalities."

Fort now stared openmouthed at Endure, who pawed the ground uncertainly.

"It is the dragons who represent the core principles. The fairies are there to help their eggs hatch, and, when a dragon egg is laid, a fairy goes to the planet to pick a scholar knight for it. Together, the knights and the dragons defended the principles they stood for and tried to make the world a better place." Kepler's tail twitched. "Your world truly is an interesting place. I found it almost as interesting studying it as I did Earth. I don't think the other scientists took quite the same view as I did. But it certainly was fun. Unfortunately, the astronomers were jealous of the power and prestige brought to the knights by the dragons. And they wanted to study the dragons. How did they fly? How did they produce fire? Understandable questions, I might say, as a scientist."

The eggs appeared over the horizon and came drifting back towards them. Abigail gently plucked them out of the sky and set them on the ground. Everyone was so engrossed in Kepler's story that no one made a move towards them this time. With a thrill, she noticed again that one was pink, and one was blue. A lot like Rose and Bluebell. Did she have a dragon, too?

"The knights were extremely protective of the dragons and refused to let the astronomers even speak to them. The astronomers built their tower, saying it was only for observation, but they were able to figure out how to leap from the planet to the moon during a syzygy, and they stole an egg to study it."

Abigail's stomach dropped. How horrible. The dragons must have been devastated, finding their egg missing. They must have felt so betrayed. Endure gave an agonized growl. Fort glanced at her, her face an agonized mirror.

"The dragons, horrified and betrayed, thought the knights had taken one. The knights of course denied it. The dragons came and searched the castle, destroying parts of it in the process. They found the egg. The knights only saw the dragons attacking them."

Abigail thought of Aristotle and his syllogisms. How if you saw a dragon laugh, it might be because you'd tickled it, but it could also be because you'd told it a joke. It was so understandable, from both sides, how the misunderstanding had happened. The dragons thought only the knights could reach their home, and so they thought that the knights must have stolen their egg. The knights knew they hadn't, and only saw the dragons turning on them, attacking. None of them knew the astronomers could reach the red moon.

Abigail shook her head. It was so complicated. Was everything this complicated? It was so easy to misunderstand. Maybe there were still pieces of the story missing. She felt calm, though, hearing Kepler's explanation. This fit, this made perfect sense. And it was so tragic that both Fort and Endure had lived their whole lives alone and afraid, with the burden of the responsibilities they carried. She swallowed around a lump in her throat.

Kepler went on. "At first, the knights were confused, but then they fought back. It escalated into a horrible conflict between the dragons and the knights, which led to the near complete destruction of both. The knights didn't know that an astronomer had taken an egg, but they thought that the astronomers had somehow turned the dragons against them. They vowed to seal away all astronomical knowledge. The fairies and I were able to hide some of the books, but Fort found me and enchanted my book. Although the fairies managed to hide me in the castle. Eventually, all anyone knew was that astronomy was an ancient evil, and something bad had happened on the syzygy."

Fort gave a strangled nod. "That's what they told me. They would barely speak about it, though."

"I remember the knights attacking our stronghold," Endure said coldly.

Fort drew herself up. "I'm so sorry," she said formally.

"Wait, you believe me?" Kepler asked. "You've only ever thought I was an annoying, potentially dangerous astronomer demon cat."

Fort sighed. "That all makes sense. It fits. I . . . I always had questions. There was always so much secrecy. I guess I thought the secrecy was necessary somehow . . . because we were in a fight for survival." She glanced at Abigail.

"I'm sorry to you, too." She placed her sword gently on the ground. "I really did think I was protecting you."

"I know," Abigail said. "I can see why, too."

A scream followed by a gurgle echoed from far below. Abigail went cold.

"Endure, please, please will you release Hope from the cage? The water's still rising."

Endure looked from Abigail to Fort.

Fort waved her hands, and the green magic locking the dragon's wings in place disappeared.

Endure glanced at the eggs one more time. Panicked splashing came from below.

Endure spread her wings and darted over the side of the island.

Moments later, she reappeared, a golden cage clasped in her talons, water streaming off it, a bedraggled Hope collapsed on the floor.

Endure set the cage down, and gently, with precise bursts of flame, opened it.

Abigail darted in, her arms around her sister, pulling her up and pounding on her back.

Hope was still and silent.

No, Abigail thought. *I'm too late.*

Hope coughed, seawater gushing from her mouth onto the ground. Gasping, she opened her eyes and looked around at everyone. She gave a wan smile.

Abigail gripped her in a tight hug, her heart thundering.

Hope hugged her back.

*

Eventually, Hope pulled out of Abigail's vicelike grip and looked down at herself. She took a few experimental breaths and poked her stomach.

"You okay?" Abigail asked.

Hope shrugged her thin shoulders and picked a piece of seaweed out of her hair.

"I . . . I think so." She climbed to her feet but nearly fell right back over again, swaying. Fort caught her, holding her tightly by the elbow. "Okay . . . okay . . . yep, all good."

The pink egg groaned and rolled over. The air began to shimmer around it.

Endure gasped, then coughed, sending out a cloud of flame. She scooped the eggs into her talons, unfurled her wings, and took off. She swept upwards, then dove into the fortress below.

All three fairies zipped after her.

Hope pressed her palms together and lifted onto her toes. "Oh! Are the eggs hatching? I hope we didn't jostle them too much. I'm sure we didn't." She glanced at Abigail. "Baby dragons!" She sprinted after Endure, crouching at the edge of the hole and peering in.

Abigail and Fort stood alone now on the edge of the island. The wind whistled around them, and far below the waves lapped at the shore as the tide continued to rise.

Fort's hand was on her sword pommel, now sheathed, and she darted a glance at Abigail before looking down. She scuffed her boots in the dirt then straightened her shoulders and turned to face her.

"I really am sorry," she said, looking earnestly at Abigail. "I'm sorry for what I said earlier. About your intentions. I see you were trying to help."

Abigail thrust her hands into her pockets, but she smiled at Fort. "Thanks. It's okay. Things are so complicated sometimes. It's so easy to misunderstand. Especially when we're afraid."

Fort gave her an evaluating stare.

"Very true . . . You know, I'm sorry I gave you that name. I misjudged you. I think I named you based on myself rather than on you. I saw a Worry because I was worried."

Abigail shrugged, unsure of what to say. Not used to this open, apologetic Fort.

Fort suddenly stood, grabbing a handful of her hair. "Did I . . . no . . . I told them to wait to fire the weapon until I got there. Didn't I?" She looked around, but not seeing Fern, returned her gaze to Abigail. "Sorry, what was I saying?"

"Weapon?"

Fort waved a distracted hand. "I've been building canons. A lot of them. To attack the moon. We'd probably better head back in case . . . but I'm pretty sure I told them not to . . . but if I'm gone too long . . ."

That was troubling.

"But I wanted to say . . ." Fort went on. "Now that I know your name is Wisdom, I can see it. That's absolutely fitting."

"I guess worry and wisdom can look alike sometimes," Abigail said.

Fort nodded. "Very wise!"

Abigail's stomach clenched. "Thanks . . . but . . . honestly . . . can you just call me Abigail?"

"What? Why?"

"It's just . . . it's a lot of pressure. I'd rather be . . . somewhere in the middle . . . than feel like everything about me has to be a certain way."

Fort opened her mouth, then stopped herself, with a finger to her lips. She chuckled. "Fair enough. I was going to say that was wise, too. But . . . that's . . . very Abigail of you."

The tension went out of Abigail's stomach. She could just be Abigail. Not worried or wise, but a combination of both. And someone who could change every day.

"Thank you. And . . . I'm sorry I went through your stuff."

"You what?" Fort stood up straighter.

"When I got Kepler's book?"

Fort sagged. "Oh, right. Well, that's okay. All in all, I'm glad you did I guess."

Abigail twisted her fingers. "Um . . . can I ask . . . what was the medal for?"

"Medal?" Fort looked genuinely confused for a moment. "Oh. That." She waved a hand. "The capital was under attack. I figured out a way to fend off some . . . some . . . well I was going to say monsters but . . ." one hand went to her throat. "I hope I didn't misunderstand that, too." Her eyes glazed over, and she looked like she might be running through every memory she had looking for misunderstandings.

"I'm sure it was different," Abigail said hurriedly. Fort really didn't need anything else to worry about. "Umm . . . and . . .

. there's still one book missing? Einstein? Do you know where it is?"

Fort unwillingly came back to the present. "Oh. No. That one was missing before my time, I think."

"Huh. I wonder where it is . . ."

"Well, you have my permission to search the whole castle!"

"Thanks!"

"All the keys, all the doors, everything I know!"

"Awesome!" Abigail smiled warmly, deciding not to mention she already had most of the keys, then glanced up at their planet. "Um, should we go check on your canons?"

"My what? Oh! Right! Oh no. Yes, let's go!"

Gravity Simulator

There's a really cool website (*www.GravitySimulator.org*) where you can play around with gravity in our solar system. What would happen if the Earth were orbiting around Saturn? Well, it would mess up Saturn's rings! You can see the effect simulated here! (Select the Saturn's Rings simulation and then click the play button in the lower left corner.) You can also see what would happen if gravity itself were stronger or weaker. Go to the full Solar System simulation, then click on the physics menu on the right-hand side. Lower down where it says 'Gravitational Constant' try increasing or decreasing that. Notice what stronger or weaker gravity does to the orbits of all the planets! "When Galaxies Collide" is also super cool!

Chapter Eighteen:
The Ideal Number
of Kitchens

ENDURE took some heavy convincing to leave the eggs, even for the short trip back to the planet. It was a harder journey than before, now that the syzygy had passed, but the fairies helped, and soon they stood again at the top of the astronomy tower, watching Endure flap away towards the red moon.

The townspeople were thanked and sent home, and over the next few weeks, while they waited for news of the eggs from Endure, Fort began Abigail's lessons on being a Scholar Knight.

Three weeks later, Abigail sat in what had once been a kitchen and was now her workshop. Rain pattered cozily on the glass domed roof. The walls were filled with shelves crammed with tools and all the magical objects she'd scavenged over the years.

Bluebell lounged against a glass bell jar, watching as Abigail bent her head over the set of brass scales she was tinkering with. A haze of sparkly blue fairy dust floated around them. Abigail gave a brass screw a final turn, then held her hand out over the scales, screwing up her face and closing one eye in concentration.

An explosion burst outward, crackling with bolts of blue energy. It enveloped both of them and then imploded in on itself.

Abigail ran a finger over her eyebrows. They were both still there. And not on fire.

"Nice," Bluebell said.

Abigail grinned.

The door behind her burst open.

"They're coming!!"

Hope collided with her, gripping her shoulders and spinning her around. "Come on come on come on! They'll be here any minute!"

She paused, suddenly noticing the crackling of energy in the room.

"Wow, what are you working on?"

Abigail's grin widened. "Oh man, so many things!" She gestured to the scales. "This will show you the worst possible outcome on one side and the best possible outcome on the other. The more likely thing will tip the scales."

She addressed the scales. "I'm considering going outside." A whirling sound emanated from the device. An image appeared on each side. On the left, Abigail walked outside, was immediately hit by a meteor, trampled by a herd of dear, and then kidnapped by pirates.

"You survived, though!" Hope said brightly.

On the other side of the balance, Abigail went on a pleasant walk through the woods, stumbling upon a magic flower. She picked the flower. Rubies, emeralds, and gold began to spill out of it. A few minstrels passing by began to serenade her, and a group of gnomes invited her to a magical feast.

"I could see that happening," Hope said.

The side with the minstrels tipped lower. It was apparently slightly more likely than the pirate scenario. Abigail frowned. "They're both too extreme, still. I need to adjust it. I want it to be useful for people."

"That's amazing," Hope said, grabbing her arm and tugging. "Come on . . . there's one more kitchen, and Fort needs our help."

Reluctantly, still thinking about how she would adjust the scales, she let Hope drag her away.

They sprinted past the library and down a corridor, a herd of kitchen implements at their heels. A kitchen doorway tried to hide unobtrusively behind a large potted plant, but Abigail saw it.

She waved a hand and with an explosion of blue fairy dust and the sound of harp strings, the kitchen turned back into a music room.

"You're getting good at that," Hope said.

"I mean, the castle's given us a lot of practice," Abigail said.

A large crash followed by several bangs and a shout drew them up a set of steps towards the old classrooms.

Fort lay frowning under a pile of stainless-steel pans. With a clatter, she pushed the pile off her. She waved a hand at it, and the pans turned into handkerchiefs, then ceramic mushrooms before merging with the floor tiles below. The stones now had a pretty mushroom design.

"Fern, did I remember to put the timer on for the cake?"

"Yes, you did."

"And the—is the turkey fully defrosted?"

"As of last night. Fully defrosted and in the oven!"

Her hands went to her head. "The crumpets! I think those were in the kitchen that we—"

"No, no, we moved those to the other kitchen before you vanished that one."

Fort let out a long sigh. "I'm glad you're keeping track of things." She caught sight of Abigail and Hope. "Ah, girls. Wonderful. I'm glad you're here." She stood, brushing herself off. Fern gave a cheerful wave. "This kitchen is particularly troublesome, and our guests will be here any moment. Could you give me a hand?"

They lined up facing the arched doorway. Abigail narrowed her eyes at the mint green rows of cabinets and innocent pastel pink table and stove. This was the strangest one yet.

It'd be no match for the three of them, she was sure.

They locked elbows.

There was a groan and a magical explosion. A cloud of pink, green, and blue fairy dust cleared.

The kitchen wavered slightly but was otherwise unchanged.

Something scuttled in one of the cabinets, followed by a muffled "Shh."

Abigail raised an eyebrow and darted inside. She threw open the cabinet door, Fort and Hope right behind her.

Silverware and cooking implements scuttled away, hiding behind a large, leather-bound book. A fork peeked out from behind it.

Another group of silverware held a tablecloth stretched flat between them. On this cloth rested several glowing balls, making indentations in the smooth surface of the cloth.

"Oh, they're reading!" Hope said.

"It's the last missing book!" Abigail said. "Einstein?"

A glowing head poked out from around a corner of the cabinets. "Oh, um, yes?"

Fort gasped and leapt backwards. Her sword rang out as she drew it in one quick movement. "Astronomers!"

Abigail held up her hands in what she hoped was a calming gesture. "It's okay, Fort!"

Fort took a few deep breaths, her hand pressed flat to her chest. She lowered her sword point a few inches but watched the ghost and the kitchen utensils warily. A few of them crawled out from behind the book.

Abigail addressed the ghost. "What are you doing here?"

The ghost ran a hand through his shock of poofy white hair. "Oh, well, these fellows had questions for me. I was just showing them about how matter bends the space around it." He pointed at the tablecloth. "Those glowing balls are like planets, you see? If you put a marble on there, it would roll into those little indentations the balls make. That's how gravity works."

177

Abigail had thought she'd fully understood gravity after talking to Newton about it, but apparently there were yet more and more layers. "Wow . . ." she said. "Umm . . . why?"

"That's the question!" Einstein said happily.

"Well, would you mind moving out of this kitchen for now? We want to turn it into something else."

"Oh, certainly, of course." Einstein said. Then he looked down at the book and at his own ghostly hands. "I don't suppose you could . . ."

"I've got it!" Hope gently scooped the book up, sending some spoons scurrying away.

Fort was taking long, slow, deep breaths behind them.

Kepler popped out of the ceiling and Fort flinched.

"They're here!" he said. "Oh, Einstein, good to see you."

"Johannes Kepler! Fantastic to see you as well." Einstein turned to Abigail and Hope. "What an absolute giant in the field, let me tell you. I'm a great admirer."

Kepler smoothed his moustache.

Fort cleared her throat, and they all turned to look. Her face was slightly pale, her jaw tense.

"Would you . . . care to join us? We are having a bit of a party."

Kepler's eyes widened and his tail twitched.

"I would be delighted, thank you," said Einstein.

"Galileo will be there!" Hope said.

"He will?" Abigail asked.

Hope waved a hand. "Oh yeah, you talked about how helpful he was. I thought we should invite him! I went over there and brought him back!"

"Oh! That's great! He'll be so happy to see you all," Abigail said.

A knock rang through the castle, accompanied by a series of chimes and gongs.

A thrill went through Abigail's stomach, and they all made their way to the great entrance.

There on the stone threshold stood Endure. Somehow looking even bigger and more powerful here on their small entryway courtyard. On either side of her were two tiny dragons: one pink, one blue.

"This is—" Endure began formally, but the tiny pink dragon was already a tiny pink blur making a beeline for Hope. It twirled around her feet a few times, crawled up to the top of her head, down one shoulder, then fell off doing somersaults. It sprinted back to Endure, then back to Hope, where it paused at her feet, staring up at her with large wide eyes, its head cocked to one side. "—Aspire. Aspire, this is Hope."

Aspire chirped and flapped up to perch on Hope's silver head. Hope laughed and patted it.

The blue dragon made its way sedately over to Abigail. Its name somehow found its way straight into Abigail's mind. "Hello, Discern," she said. It examined her cooly with its sapphire eyes. She suddenly had a vision of them flying together, years and years in the future. They were going to go so many places, do so many things. She couldn't wait.

But now, it was time for dinner. Everyone except Endure, who was too large to fit inside but would stay on a specially prepared balcony outside, went inside to the largest and best of the remaining kitchens.

Fort, Abigail, and Hope, with the help of the enchanted kitchen, had prepared a large feast with everything they or the baby dragons could want.

Discern spent most of the dinner calmly exploring every inch of the kitchen, poking into every cabinet and evaluating every cauldron and bundle of herbs. Aspire built herself a nest of Hope's hair and remained perched atop her head. Galileo set up a telescope at one window and spent most of the dinner deep in conversation with Einstein.

Abigail mostly sat quietly by herself, eating two warm, flaky pieces of bread with the thick stew Fort had made. Her stomach felt warm and full, and not just from the food. She watched her sister chatting happily, and Fort's shoulders slowly creeping down from her ears as she began to finally relax.

Kepler hopped up onto the bench next to her and she scratched him behind one ear.

"How's it feel?" he asked.

"Nice," she said.

"Nice to be able to finally do magic?"

"Yes, but you know, I think it's more that there was something not quite right in the whole castle. Fort was so scared; Hope was having to do it all herself . . ."

"I was constantly spouting sea facts . . ."

"Those were pretty interesting, honestly."

"Well, I'm glad to hear it, because do you know what's better than sea facts?"

She soaked up the last of the gravy in her bowl with a crust of bread and glanced at him. "What?"

"SPACE FACTS!" He lifted onto his hind legs and waved his front paws.

She laughed and took a bite of the bread. "Oh yeah? Like what?"

"If you connected the sun to our planet with a giant string, then as our planet moves, it would sweep out little wedged-shaped areas, right?"

Abigail frowned, chewing. "I think I could see that."

"Well, for any given amount of time, the area swept out would be exactly the same, no matter where the planet is in its orbit."

She tried to picture this. "Huh. That is pretty interesting."

"And did I ever tell you about the supernova I observed?"

"No, I don't think you did."

"Of course not! I was enchanted! Well, no time like the present. So . . . do you know what a supernova is?"

Abigail shook her head.

Kepler's eyes lit up. "Well! Let me tell you . . ."

Abigail listened as Kepler talked and talked, letting the warmth of the food and the cozy glow of the kitchen and the happy murmur voices all around lull her into a comfortable sleepiness.

She was happy to be here with the people she loved. Happy to have her own name without the pressure or expectation to be either anxious or wise. Happy to just be herself.

Gravity Writing Prompt:

Look back at your answers to the writing prompt at the end of chapter one. Spend 5 minutes journalling about what you've learned about gravity. Feel free to write whatever thoughts come to mind, or to use any of these questions to guide your thinking: Was there anything about gravity that's different than you thought? Were your thoughts similar to those of any of the scientists? (Aristotle, Kepler, Newton, Galileo, or Einstein?) What is your favorite fact about gravity?

THE END

Thanks for Reading!

✦

Thanks so much for reading, I hope you enjoyed the book!

If you have a moment, I would greatly appreciate an honest review on Amazon.

If you'd like more physics stories, worksheets, and games, you can check out my website: www.MathwithSarah.com.

One super fun free activity that's related to gravity is Starlight Starship: An Interstellar Voyage of 3-D Shapes and the Inverse Square Law. You'll find it on the books page!

Or you can try a free demo of The Sorceress of Circuits: A Steampunk Electricity Adventure on the games page!

You can also sign up for the Sometimes Science newsletter, where I sporadically send out updates about what I'm working on, free resources for learning physics in fun, hands-on ways (preferably in stories), and the occasional meteor shower heads-up.

Physics Fables Sneak Peek!

Physics Fables is an illustrated collection of short stories that teach physics concepts ranging from special relativity to magnetism for ages 8-10!

Sakura and the Many-Layered Sea:
A Tale of Density and Buoyancy

Once upon a time, on the oily shores of the Many-Layered Sea, there lived a girl named Sakura. You might think that an oily sea sounds worrisome, as if it were the result of a spill or disaster, but this was simply how the sea was. The top-most layer was a quarter-mile thick of oil and plentiful with swarms of oil eels. Which were delicious.

Sakura had short, straight black hair, wore little pink shell earrings, and was fascinated by the sea, as she was fascinated by many things. She had so many questions, but she could barely get them out because she was listening so hard, taking in all the information around her.

One night, she and her grandmother were up late repairing fishing nets. Winds moaned around the corners of their

little house, and the drumming of the rain on the roof drowned out all but the loudest cracks and pops from the fire.

"The sea dragon is angry with us today," her grandmother muttered to herself.

Sakura had never seen the dragon who protected the sea, but her grandmother often blamed him when the storms came up.

"Why is the dragon angry with us?" Sakura asked.

"Because we have taken too many of his eels," her grandmother said. "We try to limit how many we take, but this time of year there isn't anything else to eat."

"That doesn't seem fair," Sakura said.

"His duty is to protect the sea creatures," her grandmother said calmly, and for a while they sat in silence, listening to the rain pound like fists against their home.

"Tell me again," Sakura said, struggling with the unruly fibers of the netting. "Who lives below the oil?"

Her grandmother smiled, the firelight flickering off her glasses, but she didn't look up from her work. Sakura marveled as her grandmother's knobby fingers flew deftly across the fibers, untangling and repairing at a blinding pace.

"Below the oil is where the mermaids live, of course."

"And they will grant you wishes?"

"To a lucky few, yes," her grandmother said, twisting two strands of rope together. "Or that was how it used to be. They left in my own grandmother's day. They went to the center of the Many-Layered Sea, where the dragons go to dance, and no one has heard from them since."

"Why did they go?" Sakura asked.

Her grandmother shook her head. "No one knows."

"Then how do you know where they went?"

Her grandmother laughed. "I don't know. That's a good question. Maybe they told us why they left, and we didn't listen. Or maybe they didn't go there after all."

Sakura considered this, then jumped at a crack of thunder overhead.

The next morning, Sakura went out with her father to fish for the oil eels. Rain still poured from the sky in great sheets that sank into the oily waves, descending in great droplets to join the water layer far below. Sakura stared over the side of the boat, her nose close to the shiny surface as the thick waves slowly heaved and ebbed.

No shimmering shadows of eels today. She squinted, trying to make out the water below the oil, straining for a glimpse of a long-nosed mermaid looking back at her, or a flick of tail, but there was nothing. There were other, thicker layers below that, with unnamed armored creatures lumbering through it, she had heard, but she had never seen them either.

Science Note:

The Many-Layered Sea has a layer of oil on top and water below that. Why is the oil on top? Oil floats on water because it is less dense. What is density?

Well, if you had two buckets, one full of water and one full of oil, the bucket full of water would be heavier. Because the water is heavier, it ends up below the oil.

Density is the amount of stuff a given size object contains. Imagine taking a slice of cake and squishing it into as small of a ball as possible. You're packing it more tightly, which increases the density!

They caught only a single eel that day, and the next they caught nothing. For the next two months, barely anyone in the village caught anything.

The storms worsened. Great bruised clouds bubbled up, crackling with electricity and sending torrents of rain to be caught by the wind and blown into eyes and faces and open doorways. The whole village huddled together in the great meeting hall.

"We have to stop catching eels," her grandmother said, speaking in front of a crowd of elders. "We will only anger the sea dragon further."

"I haven't had anything to eat in three days," a young man said. "We have to catch something!"

Sakura raised her hand, but no one noticed her.

"We must be patient," an elderly man with a long beard said. "If the dragon sees we are obeying his laws, he will send more eels."

Sakura lifted her hand higher and waved it a bit. The eyes of the elders slid over her, like eels sliding over rocks.

"The sea dragon only cares about sea creatures. He won't take pity on us," the hungry young man said.

"Why don't we ask the mermaids for help?" Sakura cut in, unable to hold back, jumbling her words together until the room filled with a tiny beat of silence.

The silence stretched longer. A few eyebrows lifted. One or two of the elders glanced at Sakura's grandmother.

Sakura frowned. It was a better idea than doing nothing.

"Thank you, Sakura. Why don't you go home and tend the fire for me?" her grandmother said.

Sakura left the villagers arguing behind her, but instead of going home, she went to the rocky shore and stood, squinting against the rain, her hair tossed and tangled behind her by the gale. The waves swelled and crashed against the shore, filled with dark shadows of seaweed, but no eels.

There might not be mermaids out there.

The mermaids might already be gone.

She wrapped her arms around her empty belly, shivering.

If they did nothing, the sea dragon might take pity on them and send them enough eels to live. But maybe the sea dragon had decided he didn't want them eating his eels anymore.

Trying to catch more eels didn't seem like it would work, either.

193

Lightning stabbed down from the clouds like an angular trident.

She ground her feet into the smooth pebbles of the shore, listening to the crunch. Then she spun around in a whirl of pebbles, making for the docks.

She unlashed her small wooden boat, tossed the rope in, and jumped in after it. Her hands went through their familiar dance as she heaved up the mast and hoisted her coral-pink sail, webbed like the fingers of a gecko.

Thunder rumbled as she crashed through the swelling waves of oil. It splashed over the sides of her boat, and soon her fingers were slippery with it. The rain beaded up on her skin and trickled across it.

"I'm going to find the mermaids," she whispered to herself. But what if there weren't any mermaids, after all?

Science Activity:

 To see density in action, grab a cup or bowl, a scale, some gravel, and some sand. Fill the cup with gravel and place it on the scale. How much does it weigh? Now, leaving the gravel, pour sand into the cup around it. What happens to the weight? By filling in the empty spaces of the cup, you've increased the density! The cup remains the same size, but it's more tightly packed, so it's heavier!

Sakura piloted her tiny craft up and down the waves for many hours until her stomach heaved along with the waves.

At first, she thought she might be imagining it, but a great rushing sound built and built, like a river heavy with snow-melt cascading over a cliff.

A spiraling whirlpool appeared a few hundred feet from her boat. It whirled faster and faster, and she could see the funnel extending deep into the oil, all the way to the water layer below. At last, in a great spray of water, a fearsome dragon with long whiskers appeared. He bared his golden teeth at her, his eyes flashing like the lightning behind him. Sakura cowered in her tiny boat, crouching behind the mast, and stared up at him wide-eyed. It was the sea dragon himself!

"Go back, Sakura," the sea dragon said, his voice washing over her like powerful waves that could crush her into the sea floor.

She clasped her hands and bowed, attempting to be as mannerly as she knew her grandmother would recommend. "Hello great sea dragon. It is an honor to meet you. I apologize for disturbing you, but my family is hungry, and I have to do something. I know you don't want us to eat your eels, so I am going to ask the mermaids for help in finding something else to eat."

"Your family disobeyed my wishes." The cold winds whirled around him, lifting his many long whiskers. His long scaly body whipped and curled in the wind like a ribbon.

From her respectful bow, Sakura noticed a tiny creature with large, luminous eyes hovering at the sea dragon's shoulder.

"I apologize for my ignorance, oh sea dragon, but . . . who is that?" She pointed.

"That is Clyde," he said in his booming voice.

Clyde waved tentatively.

She waved back, and the sea dragon frowned, his moustache drooping with displeasure.

"He is my assistant." The sea dragon cleared his throat and resumed his threatening expression. "Go back to your family." With a crack of thunder, he disappeared.

Sakura couldn't go back to her family. She already knew the dragon was angry at them. She readjusted her sail and continued on.

The waves rose higher and higher, and she thought she could hear the sea dragon's growl in the whistling wind.

Lightning struck her mast, and her beautiful sail disintegrated into flames. She quickly patted the flames out with a heavy cloth. She knew better than to toss fire into the Many-Layered Sea.

Her sail was destroyed, so she pulled out her oars and rowed.

The air grew colder and colder. Her breath rose in clouds, and the rain turned to swirls of snowflakes like the cherry blossoms that were her namesake.

The cold made the oil thicker and thicker, and rowing became very difficult, but Sakura pressed on.

"Interesting," she thought. "The water freezes before the oil does."

Science Note:

Different materials freeze at different temperatures. It's why we put salt on roads. Saltwater freezes at a colder temperature than water without salt.

At last, the oil froze solid. Sakura sat for a few minutes, straining against the oars, but finally she stood, stepped out onto the frozen surface, and pried her boat up out of the ice. There was a small, boat-shaped indentation in the oil.

"Interesting," she thought again, despite the cold and her exhaustion. "I wonder what makes the indentation exactly that size." She'd seen boats laden with goods that were lower in the water. She could imagine that the heavier boats would make a larger indentation.

She put her boat on her back like a turtle shell and trudged up the slippery, frozen surface, shivering. At the crest of a wave, she set her boat down and made a sled, sliding down into the next trough, where she picked it up and trudged up the next hill.

Night fell, and she slept in her boat, shaking with cold and listening to the soft flakes of snow collecting around her . . .

I hope you enjoyed this excerpt! You can find the rest of Physics Fables on Amazon!

About the Author

SARAH ALLEN was a math and physics tutor for twenty years before becoming a full-time fantasy writer. She earned her undergraduate degree in physics with both college and departmental honors from the University of Washington, and a master's degree in cognition and learning from Columbia University.

Her all-time favorite book is *The Phantom Tollbooth*, and her current goal in life—besides growing a few flowers that aren't eaten by deer—is to write the kinds of physics books she would have loved as a kid.

Made in the USA
Monee, IL
13 November 2024

70084987R00115